Callahan's Way

~

Jack Tetirick

Writers Club Press

San Jose New York Lincoln Shanghai

Callahan's Way

Published by Writers Club Press
an imprint of iUniverse.com, Inc.

For information address:
iUniverse.com, Inc.
620 North 48th Street
Suite 201
Lincoln, NE 68504-3467
www.iuniverse.com

ISBN: 0-595-10018-X

Printed in the United States of America

For Erin

Contents

Life is what you make of it. Not one bit more, not one bit less.

A Fountain of Blood

Christina George was fourteen years old and she was bleeding to death. I couldn't believe it. Everybody stood there with stupid looks on their faces.

Moments earlier, from the doorway of Emerson Hardware I had paused to watch her race down the Main Street sidewalk on her roller blades, long tawny hair flying past her face as she darted quick defiant glances over her shoulder at the others trying to catch her. She laughed as she swept past me, just another bystander. I jerked my broom out of the way in order not to trip her. The three kids behind her were never going to catch up, she was winning her race no matter where the finish line might be. Then, in an awful split second, I saw her feet tangle and she plunged headlong through the store window with the terrible sound of splintering glass and the scream of a woman who was standing beside the window.

My broom clattered to the pavement as I rushed inside. She lay on her back among the broken glass and the litter of the window display, a jagged gash in her jeans from crotch to knee. A huge sliver of glass was buried in the center of the quivering flesh. Its point pulsated in the midst of a fountain of blood where the white skin parted.

Howard Emerson…transfixed behind the counter…stared stupidly. Gawking customers pressed closer to her then snapped back from the spray of blood. I knelt beside her and the spray passed across my face

1

like a sprinkler. I grabbed my bandana from the hip pocket of my jeans to wipe my face, but when the next huge spurt gushed out I wrapped up my fist, snatched out the piece of glass and pressed my fist into the wound. Blood sprayed again on my face as I forced my knuckles deeper. The blood in my mouth tasted like salt. I pressed down harder. Blood oozed around the bandana, but the torrent stopped. I looked up. Howard Emerson's look of shock was replaced by a sneer.

"Call the squad," I yelled. My body shook, I was sure the bleeding was going to start again. Emerson came to his senses and rushed for the telephone.

Excited onlookers crowded into the store or stared through the shattered window. Three firemen shoved their way inside, one crunched down beside me in the broken glass. When he grabbed my arm, blood boiled up ominously around my clenched hand. "Leave it there!" he commanded.

He stood up, shaking splinters of glass from his trousers. "You're part of her now, mister. Make every move like you're a part of her body." I swallowed hard. My stomach squirmed and my skin crawled as I broke into a sweat. Think about something else! *Anything* else so I wouldn't throw up.

They loaded us into the rescue ambulance with my fist still firmly planted in Christina's leg. I lurched against the side wall as we screeched away from the curb, fell across Christina's body as we careened around the corner onto Sandusky Street and slammed back again at the corner of Mad River Drive. Through the glass partition beyond the head of the stretcher I watched the driver and the other fireman in front laughing, sharing a private joke as they glanced back where I crouched beside her body. I concentrated on Christina's leg.

I knew her, of course. She was just a kid, in and out of the store, always friendly. She was pretty, a spray of freckles to go with the chestnut hair, quite a looker for a kid, even with her eyes squeezed shut. Another wave of nausea filled my stomach. I gritted my teeth and squeezed my belly muscles to fight off the urge to let it all go. I concentrated on counting backwards from how old she was. It worked out that she would have been in middle school when I was thrown off the football team. The wave of nausea passed , but now my fist was numb. I stared at it, to make sure it didn't move. Christina opened her eyes and tried to smile at me. I swallowed hard and looked out the rear windows at the trees flashing past on Mad River Drive. The huge fireman squatting in front of the rear windows held the cart firmly and watched me closely. The siren screamed from the roof above us.

***

The hospital was ready. The driver and his assistant slid the cart out of the ambulance onto the entryway while the third fireman pinned me against the cart with hairy forearms until my feet were firmly on the ground.

A hard commanding voice cut through the noise and confusion of the emergency entrance. It was Walter Pace. We all knew him, even me. His voice wasn't loud, but had an edge like sharp steel. "Straight to the OR! Don't even slow down. You…kid," he snapped, pointing toward me, "don't do anything different until you see me in the operating room." He twisted quickly out of the way as we rushed down the hallway toward the elevators.

Several nurses and orderlies pressed back against the wall. One of the nurses pointed at me, whispering to the other one. Then they laughed. I tried desperately not to stumble. The back wheel of the cart kept hitting the heel my shoe as we ran. If it caught me just right I'd trip! Then the elevator doors closed, and the firemen and I pressed around the cart in the tight space. One of the firemen snapped, "Hold your head back, kid. That sweat running down you face is going to drip on the girl." They seemed to think this was some sort of joke.

The third floor was silent after the noise of the street and hallway. Huge double steel doors slithered open and a gloomy room was suddenly brilliant with reflections from steel and glass under the glare of a huge overhead spotlight. On large metal tables instrument packs were ripped open. Nurses rushed in and out.

Christina's blood-soaked jeans and panties were cut away by a tall nurse using huge shears. She winked at me as she pulled them off. I kept trying to look somewhere else. Then they lifted her over onto an operating table, the blood boiling around my fist as I moved with them. I pressed harder trying to make it stop. Two nurses splashed water to wash off the blood, soaking my front as it ran off, then they scrubbed her skin with brown fluid that smelled strongly of iodine. The waves of nausea were stronger. My stomach retched.

A girl about my age wearing a green gown brushed past me, inserting a needle in Christina's hand, snapped two pieces of tape over it and hung a bottle of fluid on a metal tree. A large red-faced man trundled in a square metal machine, followed by a strutting doctor wearing a white lab coat over his scrub suit. The doctor barked orders at the first man and everyone else as he sat down behind his machine.

I stared at Christina's face. Her mouth moved as she watched me but she made no sound. Her gaze worked down my arms, and her eyes closed. She *knew* what I was doing. Another wave of nausea swept me as her eyes opened and rolled around crazily. They were shoving a tube down her throat. She gagged violently. Just what I needed! I clamped my eyes shut!

When I looked she was asleep. The bossy doctor was sitting on a wheeled stool, sliding here and there, watching the tubes and bottles as he fiddled with the dials on his machine. Had he ever been scared or sick at his stomach in the operating room? Probably not. The machine sighed, and Christina's chest moved up and down with the sound.

They worked around me as if I was dirty, or contagious. Walter Pace entered the room followed by a young woman. Their hands and arms were freshly scrubbed and water dripped from their elbows. They wore masks. Both surgeons were handed towels by a scrub nurse and then quickly stepped into green gowns and snapped on gloves. Pace stepped up beside me, careful not to touch me.

"OK, son," Pace said gently. "You've done your job, now step aside and we will do ours."

I pulled away and the fountain of blood burst out anew. Some of it splashed on the overhead operating room light, and some of it all over my face. "Well," said Pace, "pretty good pressure."

I was hustled out of the room by one of the nurses. I vomited all over the bloody cart sitting in the hallway.

***

An hour later Walter Pace stepped into the waiting room. I could see him through the open door of the nurses' lounge where, after a shower, two nurses had left me dressed in a scrub suit and sitting in a recliner with a huge piece of pie. They'd threatened to burn my bloody jeans and sweatshirt. They seemed to think the whole thing was funny.

Pace looked tired and his face was pale. Christina's parents stood up to meet him, their faces a mixture of fear and worry. I'd seen them a lot around town. Harold George was a quiet guy, worked at the Honda plant. Alice George was a real looker, slender like Christina, and we all knew her well. She bullied the Chief's cheerleaders into shape every fall, and taught a special class for the "emotionally impaired". Meaning guys like Loser Swopes who'd stuck a lead pencil up Freddy Sim's ass for looking over Swopes' shoulder to see why he'd flunked a test.

Alice George contrasted sharply with her quiet husband. She was as tall as Harold with easy movements much like her high-spirited daughter. She was holding her hand against her cheek, as if to shield herself from something she didn't want to hear. "My God, Walter, Chris is all right, isn't she?"

"Christina's fine," Pace snapped. "She's fine, the leg is fine, everything is fine. Good as new in several weeks." The same edgy metallic voice. He looked around the room. "Where's that kid?" He looked back at Alice George. "You better sit down, Alice, before we have to pick you up from the floor. Now maybe you know how your folks felt when I took your appendix out."

"That was different, and you know it." But relief flooded into her face. "You better sit down too, Harold," said the doctor. He looked around the room again. "Where did the Callahan kid go?" he demanded.

A hospital volunteer who managed the waiting room glared at the surgeon. "The *young man*," she said crisply, nodding toward the nurses' lounge, "became ill. I think the nurses took him off for a shower and some fresh clothes."

Alice George pushed back a strand of hair from her damp face. A handkerchief was twisted around her fingers. "What about her leg? Will her leg be normal?"

"Alice, the artery had a two inch slit in it that was as clean as I could have done with a scalpel. After we got the vascular clamps on the artery I cleaned it up and closed it with about a dozen stitches. There was nothing to it. It will heal as good as new. The Callahan boy saved her, not me."

At the mention of my name, she glanced across the hallway in my direction. "Walter, what's going to happen to that poor kid?" she asked. She was talking loud because she was so upset. Another glance at me. "People in town want to hang him on the nearest lamp post." I looked the other way. Boy, she had that right! Howard Emerson would be selling beer and hot dogs at the lynching, if it came to that.

"Not a damn thing, Alice," snapped Pace. "Not if I have anything to say about it. Especially now."

How could that steel-hard voice come out of that skinny body? He looked like a stiff wind would blow him over. He rubbed his chest briefly. "You two wait here 'til Christina wakes up. Quit worrying," he insisted. "I'm going to see that Callahan boy."

Pace stamped across the hallway. I tossed the pie plate aside and stood up, scattering crumbs. He waved me back into the seat. "I see they cleaned you up, Callahan."

"Yes, sir." The muscles in my face tightened. Always happens when someone makes me nervous. Walter Pace made me nervous. He was so damned sure of himself, as if nobody ever dared to contradict him.

"Well, Callahan, you saved that girl's life, not me. I suggest you hit the books pretty hard in school, and come see me some day. I'm getting tired of all this excitement." Pace stared me up and down, missing nothing, even the crumbs all over the front of the shirt. "And it looks as if you're just getting started."

"All I could think was I didn't want her to die," I mumbled. "And I knew if I fainted or threw up or something, she might. I've never been so scared in my life."

I felt the sweat popping out again.

"Hell, Callahan, we're all scared most of the time. Better get used to it. Makes for a good surgeon."

Why was he making fun of me? It didn't fit. There was no way he could be serious.

"You don't know much about me, Dr. Pace. I'll never be any surgeon." It was silly even talking about being a surgeon. Hardware store clerk was about as good as I was ever going to get.

Pace didn't change his expression at all, just stared as if I was a moron or something. Then he leaned closer to me. "I know *all* about you, Callahan, just like everyone else in this town. Let me tell you something. I know when the stuff's in there to make a surgeon. And I don't want any smart-assed kid telling me my business."

He was rubbing his chest again and wincing. After several seconds he started in on me again with that same clipped go-to-hell tone. "You're not going to jail, and you're not going to back down from anyone in this town who thinks you should."

A lot he knows, I thought. I'm as good as in jail right now, nobody ever got a break from Judge Woodruff, and I wouldn't ask Woodruff for a bucket of water if my hair was on fire. So what does Walter Pace know, anyway?

Pace just continued to stare as if he was reading my mind. "I want you to go in there and let Alice George have a word with you. If she starts bawling, don't run off. She needs to get over this. And as far as I am concerned, it's over." Pace scuttled quickly out of the room, still rubbing the area over his heart. I brushed the crumbs from the front of the scrub suit and walked slowly over to the visitor's room.

Harold George shook my hand, looking embarrassed and grateful. Alice George, tears rimming her eyes, put her arms tightly around my neck. Her body trembled as she held me. Felt strange. I'd never had anybody hug me that hard. She pressed her wet cheek against my face. The way she was holding me made me realize Harold George was a very lucky guy.

"Matt, how can we ever thank you?" she whispered. I shrugged and started to speak, but she put a finger across my lips. "Matt, don't make light of it. We won't forget. Ever."

I wanted to believe that. More than anything I wanted to believe it. It wasn't just Alice George hugging the way no one had ever done before; it was the way Harold George's hand had gripped me; even more, the way Christina had watched my face and tried to smile before she went to sleep. Did they really care about me? To them was I something more than the local celebrity juvenile delinquent? And Walter Pace had said…

The Stranger

Things went from bad to worse the next two weeks. The Bellefontaine Examiner ran a front page story about Christina. No surprise, it runs a front page story if a cop backs his cruiser into a telephone pole. Not much happens in Bellefontaine. The town was dying until the Honda plants moved in.

Howard Emerson was doing a slow burn. He hated publicity. It reminded everybody that he'd hired a juvenile offender. Like the store wasn't safe with me in it. He'd only hired me after Jimmy Peters put the arm on him the day after my trouble.

Jimmy Peters. A young cop. Not a big guy, about one-forty and five-ten, but all muscle. One afternoon, when he'd picked me up wanting to know why I wasn't in class, instead of busting me we went to the basement of the jail where the cops work out.

I couldn't believe him. What he did with the weights and then the calisthenics. "It's surprised a few big drunks," was all he said when I asked him about it.

I knew Jimmy was trying to send me a message. Before all of this happened, he'd taken me aside down at the trailer park where I lived with my Mom and that creep, Wallace, and tried to warn me about the older guys where I was hanging out. Also he was the one who yanked me off of Bo Wallace. A good thing. I would've killed Bo if Jimmy hadn't yanked me off him. After things settled down, and the squad had taken my mother off to the hospital, Jimmy spent the rest of the night getting me into the Logan County Foster Home over in Zanesfield instead of the jail. I heard he took a lot of heat from Judge Woodruff for that. Woodruff wants everybody in jail until he sends you to Columbus and the Corrections Center. Woodruff doesn't want juvenile criminals dirtying up his town.

So Howard Emerson was getting steadily more pissed off, especially when customers asked him about Christina diving through the window. He had the plate glass replaced after a shouting match with Bill Hadley over the insurance, and when Charlie Hire, one of the town's lawyers, asked Howard if he could handle the lawsuit, Howard went white as a sheet and started sputtering. Charlie walked out laughing. So I knew when Christina waved at me from the lawn in front of the Courthouse where the cheerleaders were practicing for the Labor Day parade, Howard Emerson was primed to blow his top.

She ran across Main Street and bounced into the store from the bright sunshine. It was hot and humid, and she was wearing her maroon and white pleated cheerleader's skirt and a white shirt. It had only been two weeks since the accident, and Howard looked at her like she was going to dive through his window again. When she smiled at him he managed a sickly grin.

"Gee," she said brightly, "this place is all cleaned up." She inspected the worn wooden floor closely. "Any of my blood still around?" she inquired.

"Of course not," replied Howard stiffly. He moved between Christina and the window. He glanced quickly over toward the courthouse lawn to see if any of the cheerleader's mothers were watching his store. Of course they were. Those women didn't miss anything.

"Mr. Emerson," Christina asked sweetly, "could Matt come outside and talk to me for a minute?"

I was suddenly very busy restocking wood screws on a shelf. Even against the bright background of the street I could see Emerson was furious. "Matt has a lot to do," he replied lamely.

"Just for a minute or two," Christina insisted. Emerson nodded and jerked his thumb at me as he walked back behind the counter.

I will say one thing about Christina George. She was just a kid, even if she was only half a head shorter than I am, but when we stepped out into the hot sunshine she was something to look at. It was her attitude, I guess… she was so full of it. Her eyes sparkled, they were greenish-blue, the sunshine danced in her hair, even the freckles seemed to glow. She started in teasing. She hiked up the pleated skirt, pointing at the long bright red scar. "See what you guys did to me?" she asked.

"Looks a lot better than the last time I saw it."

"I'll bet," she replied. She dropped the hem of her skirt and straightened up, tucking in her shirt. She was well on her way to growing a great pair of hooters. "So, Matt, where do we go from here?" she asked.

She caught me staring. Or she was a mind reader. "What are you talking about?" I mumbled.

"Well, you saved my life, Matt. Guess I belong to you, don't I?" She giggled, trying to act like she was teasing, but underneath there was a serious tone that was unmistakable.

"You've been reading too many comic books."

Christina made a face. "Say what you want, I remember the way you looked in that ambulance. I could tell. There was no way you were going to let me die."

"Christina, if it hadn't been me, it would've been a fireman, or Howard Emerson or somebody."

"Howard Emerson. Pooh! He was about to faint. You don't think I remember. I remember it all!" She smiled mischievously. "I even remember when they cut off all my clothes."

"Well, they had to do that." This kid was embarrassing.

"Of course." Christina blushed slightly. "Anyway, we're special, I know it," she said firmly. I could tell she had been thinking about this for some time. "See over there?" she asked, changing the subject abruptly

I looked toward the cheerleaders sprawled all over the grass. Christina's mother was talking to a group of women at a large round cement picnic table. "So what?"

"That funny-looking little man?"

I saw him then, sitting on the bench closest to the girls, in the shadow of the large bronze statue of Blue Jacket, the Shawnee chief who they say lived right there where the Courthouse is now. What I really saw, though, just beyond the little squirt, was where Sally Woodruff was stretched out. Now *she* is something to dry up the saliva. Dark red hair plastered over her forehead, all sweaty, deep tan everywhere, a smile you could see a block away, and a body that would wreck a semi-truck…probably had. Christina punched me sharply in the ribs. "Quit drooling, Callahan. Look at the guy," she snapped.

I tried to concentrate. He was small, wore a dark business suit, a white shirt and tie, apparently oblivious to the heat. Except for a fringe of black hair he was bald. The deer flies were after him. He kept slapping at them, and then would stare at his fingers before throwing them down on the pavement. In his other hand he held a small black notebook.

"He came and sat down right after we began practice," volunteered Christina. She was whispering, for no good reason, the traffic was making plenty of noise. "He was about four feet from me. I wondered if he was some creep, or something. You know. Rapist!"

"He looks harmless enough." He looked like he couldn't rape a rabbit. My eyes kept wandering over where Sally was all stretched out.

Christina nudged me sharply. "Erimina Woodruff, Sally's mother, must not have thought so. She flagged Jimmy Peters coming out of the courthouse, and sent him over to question the guy…Jimmy came up right behind me." Christina yanked at the front of my shirt to re-focus my attention. "The man said his name was Harold McQuirk. Said he was writing an article for the Columbus Dispatch about the Labor Day parade. But he was lying." Christina sounded like Sherlock Holmes.

"What do you mean?"

"He wasn't writing any article. He was watching Sally Woodruff...not that I blame him. Jimmy told him that Sally's father was the local judge, and 'as mean as cat piss.'" Christina giggled. "Then Jimmy asked him for some I.D., and the man refused. That made Jimmy mad. I thought he was going to arrest him."

"Jimmy can't arrest him. He hasn't done anything. Anybody can sit on a park bench and write notes."

"That must be what Jimmy told Erimina when he went back over. I saw her really chewing Jimmy out. The Judge doesn't like Jimmy anyway, Matt. He thinks Jimmy's too soft for a cop." Christina realized what she had said. "Oh, I'm sorry, Matt, I didn't mean about you. Jimmy likes you. Everybody knows that."

Was there *anything* everybody didn't know about me?, I wondered. "Christina, I have to get back to work. Howard's not happy with all of this."

"But Matt!"

"Like I told you, Christina. Lay off the comic books."

I stepped into the dark interior, but it was far too late. Howard had blown his top. I hated that. I really needed the job.

"Come in back with me, Callahan," he ordered. He marched all the way behind the plumbing supplies before he said a word. Then he turned on me. His face was flushed. There was a bit of spittle at the corner of his mouth. "What did that girl have to say?" he demanded.

"Just small talk," I replied.

"You start bragging about yourself and you're going to get me sued!" he snapped.

"We didn't talk about the accident," I lied.

"It's easy enough for you," Emerson said, starting the lecture I knew was coming. "You people down in the trailer park think money flows in from welfare...or the railroad...or both." This was a reference to the pittance my mother received after my father was killed in the switch yard.

"I get a lawsuit from that girl's family, I'm finished! Do you understand anything like that, Callahan? You don't have Wal-Mart to worry about, do you Callahan! Let me tell you this! If one word gets back to me that you have been talking about that accident to anybody, you're through here." Emerson mopped his face with his handkerchief. "By the way, when school starts next week, I'll only need you for two hours after school, that's all. No more Saturdays. This isn't any charity ward."

Howard Emerson turned and stomped back toward the front of the store. I knew he was only waiting for the publicity to die down so he could get rid of me.

Back in front I picked up several rolls of masking tape and climbed into the window display. Emerson wanted strips placed vertically on the plate glass so there would be no doubt there was a window there. Across the street the cheerleaders were hard at it again, including Alice George who was wearing Ohio State track shorts and a running bra heavily stained with sweat. Sally glistened as well, and I wasn't getting much done until the weirdo, Harold McQuirk, got up from the bench and blocked my view. He was headed toward me, paying no attention to the traffic. If he did that very often he would be writing in his notebook from a hospital bed. I ignored him, hoping to see more of Sally Woodruff in action, but as he passed my window he glanced up, staring through thick glasses. Our eyes met, his were huge behind the lenses. Then he moved on with quick short steps like he couldn't quite see the sidewalk.

A Car Thief

Never-Never Land. How did I ever end up in Never-Never Land? A misfit ugly building filled with misfits like me. A dingy three-story frame building across from the Post Office on the main intersection of the tiny village of Zanesfield, Ohio. Built as a hotel when Rt. 33 was the best way to get to Fort Wayne and Chicago, it was even uglier now after fifty years of failure; in need of paint and the sidewalk in front was tilted and cracked. The windows at street level had chunks of putty missing around the edges of the panes. Officially named the Logan County Foster Home, but known among the townspeople as Never-Never Land. The Zanesfield kids named it that...after all of the repeated warnings not to go near the place or to have anything to do with anyone coming in or out of it.

A block away life was normal. I watched the action from an open window on the third floor where I sat wondering why in the hell any of this had to happen. Out there neat cottages lined the street in both directions. Artim's General Store had a postcard appearance as did the tiny Helen Walker Park across from it. There was a soccer game in the street, cars slowed and waited until the play finished and the kids moved out of the way. No honking. Everybody waved or yelled at everybody else. Like they hadn't already seen each other five times that day. If anyone glanced up as they drove below me, they looked away quickly. Like they might catch something by staring at anybody in the place.

It was the red haze that had landed me in this dump, I realized. The red haze scared the crap out of me. It would come over me, then things happened I couldn't control. Like everyone else is frozen and I'm the only one moving, and there is this red haze in the air. Then it's over.

Sometimes something good happens; it happened once on the football field when we were losing and a guy from Marysville had just shoved my face in the mud. The coach told me later that I had called my own number and then sprinted eighty yards through the other team. But usually something bad happens, like when I took the baseball bat to Bo Wallace, my stepfather.

I heard somewhere that people with epilepsy do stuff like that. Do I have epilepsy? Or a brain tumor. Brain tumors do stuff like that to you, don't they? Who knows? All I really know, I am stuck in this crummy room with my new room-mate, Zinger Alexander, a car thief.

I watched Zinger walking toward the store to get some Coke and chips. We had agreed the dinner they served us would have made a starving dog puke. Zinger walked right through the clot of kids playing soccer. They parted as he passed and then kept playing, as if he was just a shadow or something. Nobody seemed to pay any attention. Everybody was being careful.

A shiny dark blue Lincoln pulled up and searched for a place to park among the several scattered pickups and partial wrecks on 'our' side of the corner. Walter Pace emerged, looked around to get his bearings, and entered the building with a quick purposeful step. I got up, went to the door and unlocked it, stepped out in the hallway and watched him at the lobby desk. Then he headed up the steps. He didn't look up until he was several steps from the top, when he stopped, he grasped the banister and stared down the stairwell while fighting to catch his breath.

"I could have come down," I said.

Dumb. If I'd wanted to go down, I would have already done it.

Pace ignored it. "No privacy in that lobby. We need to talk." Pace pushed past me into the room. "What a dump." He surveyed the beat-up furniture and the iron double bunk. "What low-life you rooming with, Matt?" He settled into the rocker I'd been using by the window. He was still puffing like he had just finished a race. Sweat popped out on his forehead.

"A black guy. Zinger Alexander." I replied. "They found him working in a Dayton chop shop and sent him over here. Doesn't say much."

"You'll be schoolmates?"

"Five of us from here are going over to the High School." I sat down on the edge of the lower bunk bed. "Starts next week."

Walter Pace stared out the window. He pressed a handkerchief on his sweaty forehead. "Matt, I want you to come live with me."

Well, I already knew this was why he was here. Second time I'd heard this today. Around noon, the case worker from Juvenile rushed over from Bellefontaine, pulled me out of the dining room, all hot and bothered that the great Doctor Pace wanted me to move into his big house up on Seventh Street. She said Pace had lived alone for the last ten years. Was that supposed to be some kind of record? Besides, it wasn't true. A big dog lived there too. Buck was a huge yellow Labrador who used to bark at me when I was delivering handbills. Buck was a big fake. Besides, I knew all about Pace living alone. His wife ran off with a charter-boat captain. Everybody in town knew. A local joke. There weren't many secrets in Bellefontaine. And he knew I was trailer park trash…'you people'…like Howard Emerson called us. Was I supposed to need a cure for leprosy or something by the great Doctor Pace? What made Pace think I'd live there?

"Well?" asked Pace, clearly irritated that I was daydreaming.

"The woman from Children's Services already told me."

"I'll pay wages. You can take care of the place, the lawn, the woodpile, all of that. And eat at the hospital or the Red Lantern. I'll settle with them at the end of every month."

"No thanks."

"You to listen to me, Matt." Pace shifted around to face me. "I knew your father. Your father was a fine man. He died on my operating table after that freight locomotive busted him up. The last thing he said to me was that your mother was too sick to ever work, and not to let him die. But he died anyway, didn't he?" There were streaks of sweat down Pace's face. "This isn't just about you, Matt." He paused for a moment. "I live alone in a big place. Done that ever since Francine walked out."

"I know about all that."

"Yeah, doesn't everybody. Well, can't blame her. I was never around. She went nuts in Bellefontaine. I shut my eyes to a lot of things. What does that have to do with you, right?"

I knew what was coming.

"Matt, I settle in at night with a bottle of scotch whiskey and a couple of books. Buck isn't much on the books, but he will take a lick of whiskey right quick. A man and a dog living alone get into a lot of bad habits, I guess. Well, Matt, I can still manage the whiskey and the books, but I need someone else for Buck. I think he's pretty disgusted."

"I want to get back to the trailer."

"Won't happen, Matt. I have Woodruff's promise of probation if you live with me. But it's either me or this dump, and I'm not sure if you try to stay here he won't railroad you up to Columbus. What's wrong with you, Matt? You scared of big dogs, or something?"

"Of course not. Buck's neat. I never had a dog. He barks and comes out to see me if I go past."

"He does that to everybody. Damn dog is an idiot."

"The Judge won't give me probation. He hates me. Always has, even back with the football mess. The ref wanted to forget about it. It was the Judge and the school board that kicked me off the team."

"You let me worry about Aaron Woodruff, Matt."

The stairwell outside the room creaked softly and several seconds later Zinger came through the open doorway. Zinger didn't walk, he glided. His hair was long and matted, tied in a queue hanging down his back. The sleeves of his tee shirt were cut out, showing a ripple of muscle across his shoulders. His jeans were frayed and dirty. Pace watched him with undisguised hostility.

"Hey, man," Zinger said softly, "you got a visitor, I believe." He leaned against the door jamb, the six-pack of Coke in one hand, the bag of chips in the other. "What do you say, Matt, you want me to stay or split?"

"Dr. Pace, this is Zinger Alexander. My roommate." I stood up and rested my arm on the upper bunk. "We've agreed to stick it out together. Both going to the Land of Oz."

"Where?" asked Pace.

"You know, the special class for the misfits at the school. The kids call it the Land of Oz since it's so weird and all..." Pace didn't seem impressed, so I went on. " Zinger's new around here... nobody wants much to do with people in that class..."

Pace rose slowly. The gray hair at his temples was streaked with sweat, as was the back of his shirt. He pointed a long slender finger at me as if sparks were going to jump from it. In the dim light of the single lamp there were dark circles under his eyes. Hawk-like eyes with a talon-finger tearing at me. "Matt, you're telling me because some social worker over in Dayton sends this loser here to go to school, you and he are some sort of buddies?"

I felt my face muscles tighten. Who did he think he was? The air around me faded to a dusky pink.. Several heartbeats later it was bright red. I still saw that skinny old man but the air between us was a transparent red. That old son of a bitch! I was fighting for control but the red was swirling and I was going under. Something terrible was going to happen and I felt helpless.

Out of the corner of my eye I saw Zinger. He snapped off of the door frame and faced me. He was watching me like I was a rabid animal. I knew Zinger could sense the red haze. He knew a crazy bastard when he saw one. He knew they could be lethal. That scared me.

"Easy, bro," said Zinger softly.

Pace spun around to glare at Zinger. "Is that what *you* want, Alexander? You want to head him your direction, do you?" Pace's voice trembled. He looked Zinger up and down. "You're older, aren't you ? Why don't you give this kid a chance? He could amount to something if assholes like his stepfather and you would leave him alone!"

I must admit I admired the old guy. He didn't back off from anybody. He looked like he was going to slug Zinger right then and there. But he sure must have a screw loose somewhere. As I watched him, I realized the red haze was fading. My heart was beating wildly and I felt shaky, but it was fading and nothing terrible had happened. Zinger was still watching carefully, but he had eased back against the door jamb.

"I'm staying here. I'm not going anywhere, Dr. Pace," I said. "Me and Zinger are going to do this together. And it was my idea, not his."

Pace slumped back into the rocker and stared out the window. He clasped his hands behind his head, the long slender fingers tapping on his gray hair. Several minutes passed. It was embarrassing.

Then he turned back toward us. "Well," he said, "I'll tell you what I will do. You both come. But it isn't going to be any picnic, and it isn't going to be the same for both of you." He stabbed the sharp forefinger at me again. "You have promise, boy. You may think I'm going off half-cocked, but I'm not. I've talked to your teachers. I checked you out. Coach Ebert…that poor bastard practically bawls when he thinks what he missed with you. Says you were the quickest and fastest thing he ever saw on two feet. And that young cop, Jimmy Peters. He says Bo Wallace would have killed your mother for sure if you hadn't taken that bat to him. Might have killed you too for that matter. And I know he's right about that; I've had the pleasure of patching up some of your stepfather's handiwork over the years, Matt. He never knocked anyone's eye out before, but he sure has broken up a lot of other things. He particularly likes to go for the crotch when he has a man down and helpless; uses those heavy boots he likes to show off in the bars. What he leaves after that isn't too pretty."

Pace turned then and glowered at Zinger. "So you come too, mister. Both of you come, you can eat your dinners at the hospital or over at the Red Lantern. Cut my wood and take care of my house and dog. You, Zinger, or whatever your name is, you do as you please except you better be in the house before midnight and you better stay out of trouble. But you, Matt, I want in my library every week night with schoolbooks in hand. I'll read and enjoy my fire. And you're going to stick your nose in books and keep it there until you put old Buck to bed."

Zinger walked across the room and placed his packages on the battered table by the lamp, talking with his back toward the doctor. "I don't cut firewood," he said slowly. "Don't pick cotton either. You want to make a Rhodes Scholar out of the kid, go ahead."

Pace paused and looked Zinger up and down carefully. "What would you know about Rhodes scholarships, anyway, Alexander?"

Zinger turned toward him angrily. "There you go, big man. What makes you think you know everything and people like me know nothin'?" Zinger's accent was thick. He was laying it on thick as well.

"Well, that's it boys," said Pace. "Take it or leave it. I won't be back. He walked stiffly past Zinger, ignoring him, and went heavily down the steps.

"Aw, what the hell, Matt," Zinger said quietly, "let's move in with the old boy. Gotta be better than this dump."

He ripped open the bag of chips. "Sounds like better food for damn sure. Who knows, maybe there is something over there worth ripping off."

"No stealing, " I said sharply. Why did that make me so pissed off at Zinger? There was just something about the old guy I liked…Zinger just stared. Like I was an idiot. You couldn't tell anything watching Zinger's face. He must be one mean poker player.

I yelled after the doctor disappearing down the steps. "Hey, give us a chance to talk it over!" Pace just kept going like he didn't hear me. What I really wanted to do was get out to the trailer to see if my Ma thought it was stupid for me to move up into that big house on Seventh when she was stuck down there in that crummy trailer.

Homecoming Queen

The trailer was little different than the others down the long muddy lane. Its siding was dented in several places, the entrance step was a two-by-eight laid across two cement blocks. The lower panel of the aluminum screen door was ripped open, had been that way as long as I could remember. I scraped the mud from the bottom of my Nikes on the edge of the block where it stuck out past the board. The Nikes were getting pretty beat up. I tried to take care of them, but still they didn't look like much. Last year's Christmas present. My unlined jacket didn't help much against the cold misty rain. The jeans the nurses had laundered were starting to get pretty beat up as well. I was feeling nervous about going in to see Ma. The rain made it worse.

I heard 'One Life To Live' blaring inside the trailer before I pulled open the flimsy front door and stepped into the oppressive heat. Across from the door in the tiny kitchen a spout of steam was coming from an old teakettle with a faint whistle. The warm damp air smelled like peppermint and mold.

Ma sat in her recliner facing a television propped on the narrow counter below the front windows. On the flickering screen two bodies clutched together. Sad music and sobbing. She didn't bother to look around her chair as I came in. I walked to the front and perched on the flimsy sill beside the tube. She hunched down in the recliner and glared at me. She wore the same flimsy flannel nightgown and old frayed terry-cloth robe. Her lower body and legs were wrapped in a quilt. She looked years older than her thirty-eight years. "You're not supposed to be here," she said flatly.

"Would you turn that thing down, Ma? I can hardly hear you."

A sudden silence except for the faint whistling of the teakettle. She sucked on the inhaler clutched in her right hand. I'd never seen her without it.

"I said that woman came over from Juvenile and told me you weren't supposed to be over here. Judge's orders." She sounded as if I had just robbed a bank.

"I don't care what Woodruff says. I want to see you."

"Just like Joe Callahan," Flora Jean said wistfully. "Everybody has rules but you."

"I been worried about you."

"You better worry about yourself, Matt Callahan. You're in a heap of trouble. You blinded your step-father in one eye, Matt, that's what you done. You and that terrible temper of yours."

"Ma, he was sitting on your belly on the floor with a pillow over your face!"

"He's done worse." Her eyes drifted back to the television screen. I leaned over and snapped it off. She frowned and sucked on the inhaler. The silent treatment. I felt a whiff of the red haze.

"It took an hour to get your oxygen back up to normal at the hospital. He could've killed you."

"He gets like that when he drinks. I've told you since you were four years old that you stay away from Bo Wallace when he's like that. Far as I know he never laid a hand on you except when you had it coming, and now you take a baseball bat to him."

"He's slapped you around for years. You were wheezing so bad you couldn't talk when he took the pillow away. If he comes in that door now, I'll finish the job." The red mist drifted and swirled along the hallway.

My mother fished the remote out of her robe and snapped on the television. She began to wheeze. She sucked hard on the inhaler. "You stay away from Bo Wallace. He's my husband." Her expression was hateful. "You stay the hell away from him!"

I couldn't believe what I was hearing. "Walter Pace asked me to come live up at his place."

"I heard that."

"How? It only happened two days ago?"

"Some of the hospital kitchen girls who live here told me." She glared at me, enjoying her little secrets. "I know a lot more than you think I do, Matt." She sucked on the inhaler again. "You go on up that hill and stay with Walter Pace. He might make something out of you. God knows I can't."

That's just great, I thought. When was the last time you tried?

"Pace can get to Judge Woodruff," she wheezed. "Francine, the one that run off from Walter Pace…is the younger sister of the Judge's wife…Erimina, the bitch. That old fat-assed Judge has to listen to Walter Pace. It's all mixed up in politics somehow."

"You don't like her much?"

"Who's that?"

"Mrs. Woodruff."

"She cheated me out of Homecoming Queen at the High School, Matt. She flushed some of my ballots down the toilet in the girl's locker room."

Homecoming Queen? I looked at my Ma. Skinny, shriveled, dishwater hair hanging down over a sea of wrinkles. She was watching me slyly.

"You might not think it, Matt, but I was a looker once. Your daddy thought so. Joe could've had any girl he wanted. Did have, if you want to know the truth. But he wanted me the most."

Ma's thoughts were far away. "That bitch's sister was different though," she said softly. " You know, Francine. The one…that run off from Walter Pace. She felt bad about it, we were sort of friends for awhile. I hope she's happy out there in San Diego or wherever…even if she did break poor old Walter's heart. Now Erimina's got a kid that's just like Francine...wild as a hare, spoiled rotten...you know her?" My mother watched me suspiciously.

"I know who she is, Ma, she runs with older guys. She don't know me."

"Just as well. Anyway, Walter Pace can handle Woodruff if anybody can. Him and the governor. You know about that?"

"I never heard anything about any governor."

"Pete Halliday. He's from up here. Made all kinds of money building the freeways. He's a tough customer, nobody gave him anything. Spent a lot of nights sleeping in a construction shack on the berm to make sure the concrete showed up when it was supposed to. Walter Pace and Halliday are real tight. Pace operated on Georgia a long time ago...took off her breast. She sends money every year to the Mary Rutan Cancer Clinic with a mushy note to Pace." My mother smiled at the thought. "Yeah, I have an idea that between Pete Halliday and Walter Pace, fat old Aaron Woodruff has his hands full. I understand when Halliday calls up, you don't end up wondering what it was he wanted. That's the only kind of person that fat bastard would listen to." She fumbled again with the remote, finally turning the volume up loud enough to deafen the squirrels outside. "Now get out of here Matt Callahan and don't come back! I mean it!"

All of a sudden she was shouting and wheezing at the same time. She might as well have shoved a butcher knife in my gut. All I wanted was out of there. I stormed up the narrow aisle of the trailer but before I got to the kitchen Bo Wallace wrenched open the flimsy front door and staggered in. He wore a black patch where his right eye had been, and his good eye was bloodshot. It glared at me. The smell of whiskey overwhelmed the peppermint fog. He was really loaded. He stood there swaying. I could feel the red haze settling over me. My mother was wheezing and screaming at both of us. Bo turned and stumbled back down the aisle, swerved into the bedroom and slammed the door. The whole trailer shook.

I looked back toward the front. "Bye, Ma," I managed to say. All I could see was the back of the recliner and her hand holding that inhaler.

"Don't come back," she wheezed.

I think Ma was crying. You can never tell if she is. She cries mostly to herself.

Seventh Street

Zinger and I moved into the big house on Seventh Street. He'd come up with some wheels, an old black Wrangler that looked like it had been in a fire, but the engine sounded like it belonged on a derby track. On the back seat was a pile of new clothes, including a pair of alligator loafers that cost more than the car…if he paid for any of it…I didn't ask. They don't sell anything like that in Bellefontaine, and he had been away for two days. Just showed up this morning as cheerful as if he'd won the lottery, lecturing us junior felons at Never-Never land that it was no disgrace to be poor, just stupid to stay that way.

He pulled around the back of Pace's brick drive as if he owned the place. I didn't have to tell Zinger how to get there. He knew. I thought for a minute he was going to pull the rusty old Wrangler into the three car garage between Pace's shining new Lincoln and an old red Nissan pickup, but he stopped in the parking area.

Buck wandered toward us slowly waving his big tail. He was huge with thick yellow fur and solemn brown eyes and he acted like we lived there. He went to Zinger first, then me, his expression seemed to say we were old buddies from the days of delivering advertising flyers. On one side of the large brick parking area was a brand new stanchion supporting a hoop and backboard. The cement base was still damp. What was going on? Did Pace think we were going to come out here and play basketball?

Zinger looked over the huge old oaks scattered over the half acre that was Walter Pace's yard, then turned to examine the old brick mansion. His hands were jammed into the back pockets of his new jeans. "Well, bro," he said softly, "it sure beats Never-Never Land, I'll say that."

"Morning boys." Walter Pace at the back door looked very chipper, gray hair slicked down and his face pleasantly pink, a far cry from the pallor and sweat the last time I saw him. He smiled at Zinger as if they were old friends. Zinger's face closed up tight. No expression.

"Come on in," continued Pace, holding the door open and motioning with his hand. "Get your things. Had breakfast? There's coffee in here if you're interested." Pace sounded like the guy who comes around the trailer park trying to sell magazine subscriptions.

We went back to the car and picked up our stuff. As we leaned in from opposite doors into the back seat, Zinger raised his eyebrows as he looked at me. That made me nervous. Zinger has a strange sense of humor. He gave me the same look one afternoon over at Never-Never Land, then slipped outside while the paper-boy was in the lobby and hid the boy's bike down behind the big rock at the entrance of the Trout Club. The kid came out and started screaming his bike had been ripped off, they even called a Deputy Sheriff. Finally they found it, all the while Zinger sat at the third floor window watching, and when he looked back in the room he would smile that weird smile and raise up his eyebrows.

The kitchen was huge. I never saw so much stainless steel. Even though the house must have been fifty years old, all of this stuff was the latest. A ceramic island with two cooking areas filled the center of the room. On the far wall was a refrigerator and what looked like the door to a walk-in freezer like the one I remembered at Poland's Meat Market before Kroger put them out of business.

Pace led us down a long center hall toward the front door where we turned and climbed a central stairway to the second floor. There was a front hallway and our bedrooms were down to the right. Buck padded along behind us. Sort of a parade. My bedroom was the first, Zinger's second. Pace left us.

I stared in astonishment. The bed looked wider than Ma's trailer, covered with a red striped blanket. Saw one like it in a hunting catalog once.

I threw my old gym bag on the bed. Everything I owned except what was on my back was in it, packed by Ma and brought to Never-Never Land by the social worker. Two pairs of jeans, a half dozen tee shirts, two heavy sweat shirts, some underwear and socks. Folded in the bottom was the only thing I cared about, an insulated black oiled-cotton hunting coat that Bo gave me last Christmas. I'd been offered two hundred bucks for it. If Bo didn't steal it, he knew who did.

As I crossed the room, my feet sank into thick cream carpet. I stared at the oak trees out of a long row of low windows. I ran my fingers along a desk under the window. I was too shook up to think. The wide desk had a computer and a TV on it. The sales tag was still on the TV. I even had my own bathroom with a shower. And smooth marble on the counter top.

I heard Zinger pounding up and down the stairs, bringing up his stuff. I washed my hands in the basin. No dirty cracks in the porcelain. No soap scum or curly black hairs. I washed my hands and looked at myself in the mirror. I didn't belong here. The towel beside the basin was thick and white and new. I wiped my hands on my shirt.

Walter Pace was waiting for me at the bottom of the stairway. "Matt, come in here with me for a few minutes," he said, motioning me to the library. A huge room with a massive fireplace, the walls lined with books, row after row, floor to ceiling. The lower part was all walnut doors and panels, several of which stood open showing stacks of thin white magazines. A long library table was littered with those same magazines and loose papers. Pace motioned me to a brown leather chair beside the fireplace, but I decided to stand. So he did likewise. The grate was empty. Not even any ashes. It seemed sort of dumb.

"Matt," said Pace, "there aren't many rules here, but there are a few. We need to talk about them." He sounded uncomfortable, as if I might walk out. He was right. I was thinking about it.

"What about Zinger?" I asked.

"What about him?" said Pace bluntly.

"Shouldn't Zinger be here too? Doesn't he need to hear about rules?"

"I have an idea Zinger makes his own rules, Matt. And I'm not interested whether he does or not. Zinger is here because of you, no other reason. He can stay here as long as you do, I'll pay for his board at the hospital or at the Red Lantern, the same as I will for you. Other than that he's on his own. If there's any trouble I'm sure he'll be gone. He already told me he's not interested in work. I presume you still are?"

"Yeah, I need the money. Emerson's cut me back to two hours after school. But I won't beg."

"Can you drive?"

"Sure." I was stretching it a bit. I'd taken Driver's Ed last year, but since I didn't own any wheels, I hadn't driven at all since then.

"Good. There's an old pickup in the garage. And plenty of dead timber in my woods in the country that should be cut for firewood. I want you to take Buck out there on weekends, cut up the dead timber and give Buck a good run. We used to go out there a lot. Buck misses it. I miss it too, for that matter." Pace sounded wistful. "You know how to handle a stick shift and four-wheel drive?"

"Sure." Now I was out-and-out lying. But I knew I could do it if I had the chance.

Zinger came down the stairs and flashed the bird behind Pace's back as he headed toward the back door. He seemed to know the score better than I did, without being told. I guess he'd been at it longer.

"As for the school nights," continued Pace, "as I said over at the Juvenile Home, I want you in here with Buck and me. When you finish your schoolwork, you can do as you please. You'll need some heavy clothes for the woods. Go down to Farm and Fleet and get them. I'll pay of course, and it's minimum wages for the time you spend in the wood lot."

"I'll go this afternoon, Dr. Pace," I replied. I wasn't sure I was coming back.

"Good. Make sure the pants have Kevlar facing. I don't need to be sewing up some chain-saw cut. Get heavy work gloves. You might want to clean out Buck's kennel yet this afternoon." Walter Pace seemed to be finished. He acted like he wanted to shake hands or something. Here was this guy trying to give me a break, and all it did was piss me off. But it seemed unfair, somehow, his being able to stand there and lecture me and tell me what I was going to do. He didn't know anything about what it was like where I came from, or how I felt about anything. But that wasn't *his* fault, was it?

"Thank, you, Dr. Pace," I said. It sounded really lame.

He watched my expression, amused. "Your Dad was a stubborn Irishman," he said softly. "Same size as you, same curly brown hair. Never walked away from a fight, and never started one either. Took a lot of abuse from women as well as guys smaller than he was. You're a lot like him, Matt."

"I never really knew him, "I replied. " Sometimes I think I can remember him…but I don't really think I can." That shot a pain through me. It always did.

"I know. Too bad. You wouldn't be in this mess if Joe had made it off of my operating table."

Walter Pace walked out of the room, blowing his nose hard as he went.

The Bamboo Stiletto

Are you settled in okay?" Christina babbled.

News travels fast in this town. I was hunched over a blizzard at the Dairy Queen on the corner of Hayes and Sandusky minding my own business.

"Emerson canned me except for two hours after school," I replied, watching to see whether she realized her questioning Howard Emerson about her blood all over his hardware floor was as responsible as anything. If she did, she didn't show it, she just stood there smiling with all these little kids running around like mice. All around the screened-in porch where I was trying to eat my blizzard.

"Their mothers' dropped them off," she explained sweetly. "Last swimming lesson. The ice cream is a bribe."

Christina sat down on the bench beside me, ignoring all the squealing. "So who's this guy I hear moved in with you," she asked. "Where'd he come from, anyway? One of the cheerleaders told me he's on parole or something."

I concentrated on the blizzard. This girl is a real pest!

I couldn't say the same for what I saw coming down Hayes toward us. It was a powder-blue Mercedes convertible driven hell-bent by Sally Woodruff, her hair flying behind her, everything below was dark tanned flesh except for a bikini top that didn't hide anything. As she flew into the intersection she looked up at the porch and saw something she didn't like. I knew it couldn't be me. Sally Woodruff had never looked twice at me in her life. But it sure was somebody. I saw her expression change and it wasn't pretty to see. The tires screeched as she gunned into the parking lot behind us.

"Here comes trouble," Christina muttered as she lunged to grab a plastic spoon from the dirty floor before a four-year-old could stick it back in her mouth.

I looked around. Two tables away, with his back toward us was that weirdo little guy, Harold McQuirk. I nudged Christina. "Remember him?" She nodded. He wore the same dark suit, and was spooning a sundae from a large plastic cup. A stack of napkins lay beside him. He paid no attention to the noisy kids.

Through the screen I watched Sally walk up to the counter. Guys stared at her. Well, so did I! And why not? The bikini top covered about a third of the best looking pair you would ever want to see, and the bottom was practically nothing, the back part of it was almost a thong, but not quite, maybe two inches wide. She wore bright red lipstick, several earrings, a tennis bracelet and brown shower clogs. That was it, but that was plenty. "You're drooling, Callahan. Want a napkin?" Christina patted me under my chin. I shoved her hand away.

Sally argued loudly with the kid at the service window, walked toward us and yanked open the porch screen door. She took a large bite out of a chocolate ice cream bar, wadded the wrapper in her other hand and threw it on the floor. Her eyes flickered over Christina, then me, but she was headed for McQuirk. He was two tables away and she stamped down the side opposite him. When he took no notice she stepped over the bench and sat down facing him.

We had ringside seats. "Aren't you the one who wants to play detective?" I whispered to Christina.

Sally took another bite from the bar. A loose chunk of chocolate at the corner of her mouth slid down her chin. Without looking up from his sundae McQuirk flipped a napkin at her from the pile beside him.

"You're the guy Jimmy Peters ran off from practice the other day, aren't you." Her voice trembled. "He told my mother your name is Quick or something."

"I am Harold McQuirk, Sally. Yes. Officer Peters did, as you say, 'run me off', but as you see, not very far."

A skin-headed six-year-old ran up to Christina complaining loudly that his sister had taken his money for a fudge bar. "C'mon, Sam,"Christina said, and marched off toward to counter from where the angry four-year-old stared back.

"You're waiting for me, aren't you," Sally asked. She shuddered as if suddenly chilled. I watched her face. Fear started to replace anger. She looked over at me, then back at McQuirk. Christina slid in quickly beside me, nudging me for up-to-date information. I ignored her.

"How do you know my name?" she demanded.

"You come here almost every morning, Sally," replied McQuirk, placing his spoon carefully in his cup which was now empty. The back of his bald head had a green tint from the light reflecting from the ceiling.

Sally took another large bite and ignored both the napkin and another stray chunk of chocolate that dropped onto the table. "My mother and her friends had a good laugh the way Jimmy sent you hustling off down the street."

"No doubt."

"If I tell Jimmy you're stalking me like this, he'll arrest you. My father will see that you spend plenty of time in jail!" She spit the words at him.

He didn't seem to notice. "No doubt."

Suddenly she seemed terrified. "Why are you *doing* this? I don't even *know* you!"

"I think you know why, Sally."

"No way."

McQuirk removed a napkin he had tucked over his shirt collar, stuffed it into the empty cup, leaned sideways and shoved the cup into a waste container at the end of the table. The metal lid made a loud tinny noise and Sally jumped. Then McQuirk slowly drew a small white envelope from his coat pocket, flipped it open and shook it. Something fell onto the table. Sally's face blanched, making the tanned skin turn yellow.

"What is it?" Christina hissed.

"Don't know. Can't see."

"I have a friend in Detroit, Sally," McQuirk said, " who tells me you received one of these in the mail a week ago."

Her color was coming back. "That's a lie!"

Christina nudged me in the side. I jumped. "Matt, help me get these kids out of here!" She stood up.

"Shhsh! I want to hear this."

Two kids started fighting over something at the table beyond Sally Woodruff's back. Christina ran over to them. "Stop that Susan! Quit hitting Peter!" She pulled them apart.

I was sure McQuirk heard me shush Sally. I could see his back tense, but he didn't turn around to face me. Instead he leaned toward Sally and lowered his voice…but not enough. "You owe money," he gritted. "If they don't get their money, they stick one of these things through your nose…or somewhere."

"I don't know what you are talking about!" Sally's voice rose to a shriek. "You're lying. You're trying to trick me! I'm going to tell the Judge." Sally looked across to where I was listening. Christina was busy shoving kids back into the far corner of the porch.

"No, Sally, I don't think so. You're not going to tell the Judge. If you were going to do that, you would already have done so." McQuirk took off his thick glasses. He drew out a handkerchief and polished the lenses carefully. "Nearsighted," he said, as if by way of explanation. He tucked the handkerchief away, watching Sally's face. "The thing the people up there don't like is for their employees to start using the stuff," he gritted at her. "They think it's stupid…even dangerous."

The rest of the chocolate had melted and fallen onto the table. I could see what McQuirk was seeing. Sally's eyes had been very light brown, almost yellow like an angry cat. Now the pupils were so large her entire eye seemed black. He could see how scared she was.

"I don't have any money! I need time!" She was near tears. I could tell. Or panic. "I know what you really want, McQuirk, or whatever your name is," she sobbed.

Sally stood up. His head tilted back as he watched her. She raised her arms slowly and her breasts bulged against the fabric stretching the tiny strings over her shoulders. "You would like to get your sticky fingers all over these, wouldn't you, you little creep?"

Sally reached higher, glancing quickly across at me and back to him. Sweat glistened in her armpits and ran down over the fabric. Then she leaned forward, placing both hands on the table. "Take a good look. It's as close as you will ever come." Quick as a cat she drew back and slapped him with all her strength. His head snapped sideways.

She turned and ran for the door. She jerked to a stop, twisting around and pointing at the back corner where the two children huddled against Christina's thighs. "You brought him here, didn't you!" she shrieked at her. "You told him where to find me, didn't you!"

"Stop it, Sally," Christina snapped. "I'm here with Matt! Before I take these kids to the pool for their swimming lessons. It's a free country. What are you talking about?"

"You saw him try to feel me up?" Her voice cracked and her face was contorted.

"No," replied Christina. "I didn't see that."

"What about you?" She turned and the bright yellow eyes were all over me. Top to bottom. First time she ever looked *at* me instead of through me. She ran the tip of her tongue over her upper lip. "Well?"

"I...don't know," I stammered. I wondered, was she was going to slug *me*? I was sure staring at what McQuirk got slapped for staring at.

"I…didn't see him touch you," I decided. My mouth was dry. Her gaze turned to contempt.

"If I call the cops, you better tell them what you saw, Christina." Sweat was streaming down Sally's face and there was pallor around her mouth. Her hands were trembling. She snatched one more look at McQuirk and then darted out the door. I heard the car engine roar, the tires screeched, then I smelled the burned rubber.

"Wow!" said Christina.

McQuirk stood up. He rubbed his cheek briefly as he stepped over the bench. The kids were all quiet, waiting to see what was going to happen. Then Peter started whimpering as he clutched Christina. His sister watched Peter and also started to cry. Christina pressed them back behind her, watching me to see what, if anything, I was going to do. McQuirk adjusted his coat, put the spectacles on very slowly and moved past me with his small steps. He went out of the screen door and toward the parking lot.

"Why's she want anything to do with a creep like that?" Christina demanded.

"Jesus, Christina, that guy has something on her, isn't that obvious?"

"She's freaked out. Using. I'm sure of it."

"No you don't know anything. That's the trouble with this town. Everybody thinks they know everything when they don't know anything."

I walked over where they had been sitting. Beside the mess of Sally's ice cream was a thin dark brown sliver about five inches long. I picked it up and bent it. Bamboo. One end was sliced to a needle point, edges as sharp as a razor. Isn't that just great, I thought. In two days I'll be in a class with a bunch of freaky misfits. Might as well call it a Zoo as call it Oz. And now some scary little bastard wants to make a pincushion out of the best body I have ever laid eyes on. "Matt," said Christina, "you're still drooling."

The Land of Oz

Zinger and I pushed our way past the crowd pouring from a line of school buses and climbed the three flights of stairs to Room 309...The Land of Oz. The classroom was large, but contained only eighteen chairs arranged informally before the teacher's huge desk. In the back were several library and work tables and two computers. It is reserved for us, we all know the score.

We are the 'emotionally impaired'. That's what it says on the home-room list in the principal's office. The secretary has it pinned on the wall of the office for all to see. All that is missing are juvenile records and mug shots. Why not put them up there too? I'm sure they're in a handy drawer.

Sally Woodruff is the single exception, at least for the morning class...she is allowed to leave us at noon and return to the human beings. Two of the class, both male, have ages listed as eighteen. Adults. No longer children. One of them is Zinger. Like I say, we knew it all before we ever walked into the room.

Alice George is behind the desk. As a teacher, she looks very different from the day she was rehearsing the cheerleaders. That day Howard Emerson spent a lot of time checking her out through his new plate glass window, like he'd never seen a woman in track shorts and a running bra. Today it's all business. She's wearing a yellow-striped Lands End button-down oxford dress shirt, open at the neck. On the upper edge of the shirt pocket the word "witch", is neatly stitched in black. We're in the Land of Oz all right.

Zinger and I find seats in the back. Loser Swopes…we all know Loser from the pencil-in-the-ass situation…a big kid, bordering on fat, with long straight black hair hanging down to his eyebrows, is slumped in a back row seat staring out the window. Sally Woodruff follows Zinger and me in, moves toward Loser, changes her mind and eases into a chair in the row in front of us. Her white blouse is open down the front revealing plenty of cream-colored bra. Her hair is piled up on her head and held in place with several pins with large agate heads, some kind of antiques, I guess. The effect is terrific. When she turns around to look us over, Zinger pays no attention. I do.

"You're Callahan, aren't you," she asks, after she has a good look at Zinger. I nod.

"The Judge told me all about you." If she was mad about anything that happened Saturday, she doesn't show it. When I don't say anything, she smiles at me.

"Don't worry about it, Callahan." She ran her tongue along her lips as her glance flicked again toward Zinger. "I think the Judge is full of shit." Then she turns around as the last of the students straggle in. Amazingly, before the bell stops clanging, we are all in place. Mrs. George straightens up behind her desk as the tardy bells finish off in the halls outside. "You all know me," she says simply, "you all know why you're here, I'm still trying to figure out why I am."

She doesn't sound very happy. "I don't have any degree in social work. I don't know anything about the courts or about juvenile problems. All I ever wanted to do was teach English, but with this class I'm supposed to do it all. One piece at a time. We finish one subject, we go to the next one. Nobody cares, nobody is watching. We might as well be out in the middle of the prairie. We do it all right here unless someone starts to do particularly well, in which case I have the right to send that person off to a class in the real world. I can also make one call to the principal's office and you're out on the street. That was a condition of my being here."

She opens a black notebook. "So, you all know the drill as well as I do," she says. "If you think I don't care about you, you're wrong. I care about every one of you. But I'm not going to end up in some asylum worrying about you. I repeat, do well in here, I'll arrange for you to go to classes with the rest of humanity. Otherwise you spend the year in here."

She pauses, evidently deciding whether she should say what was on her mind. "There's one person here who does not belong, in my opinion." She nods at Sally Woodruff. "Sally is here for the first three periods, as she was last year. This is something she and her father, the Judge, worked out with the principal's office. It seems Sally is going to be a lawyer and the Judge thinks she should learn her English and History in here. Well fine. Who am I to disagree with the Judge?" Her voice sounds as if she does very much disagree with the Judge.

Sally Woodruff smiles sweetly at Alice George. Christina told me the two of them fought all of last year. Christina also said the Judge, as head of the school board, resisted the idea of a special classroom in the High School, had ridiculed Mr. Rogers, the principal, for bringing the idea back from a convention. Woodruff's solution is to send anyone with a record to Columbus, but the State Board of Education finally nixed that. His compromise was to have Sally in the class for half a day. His excuse to the school board was he didn't trust Alice George not to coddle the students. He also decided if Sally was going to be a lawyer...and he had no doubt she was...'she had better start to learn early about the kind of people she would be dealing with down the line'. So Sally Woodruff spent most mornings finding new ways to bug the Witch. And Christina George kept everyone in the lunchroom informed about how it went, at least from her mother's side. Sally Woodruff had her own versions, which were a lot funnier.

Alice George looked up from the notebook. Who's Zinger?" she demanded. "We don't use nicknames in here." Zinger stirred, un-crossing his long legs and pulling himself upright. He was wearing a spotless tee shirt and narrow-legged Levis. He smiled, showing perfectly even white teeth.

"It's not a nickname, Ma'am, my momma gave it to me, I think as I was coming out." There are several snickers. Alice smiles briefly.

"Then Zinger, get a haircut. Nothing grows below the shirt collar in this classroom."

"Yes, Ma'am."

"And don't call me 'Ma'am'. Call me Mrs. George, or Mrs. Witch or whatever. I'm not anybody's Ma'am"

"I'll do that this afternoon, Mrs. Witch." Zinger sounds very serious.

Sally Woodruff looks at Zinger with new-found interest. She smiles and raises her eyebrows, showing approval that he had stiffed the teacher. Zinger looks through her at the blackboard beyond.

"I see you're back, Wilbur," says the Witch, looking toward the window.

"Loser, Mrs. George. I like the name Loser a lot better. Nobody calls me Wilbur no more."

"I do, Wilbur," she replies. Loser goes back to staring out the window. She searches the list further. Then she looks up and across at me. "My list says you're in court this Friday, Matt."

"So they tell me."

"I want to talk to you before you leave today."

"Sure."

I wondered what that was all about. Sally Woodruff watched me, amused. There had been several nasty fights over her, and I could see why, her eyes flashed yellow-brown, and that body twisted in ways that makes you feel strange. She looked straight at me and her eyes bored in. I felt myself flushing.

"You're not going to any court on Friday," Sally said softly. Her voice was husky, almost a whisper. "The Judge is going to postpone all of that. I heard him yelling at Uncle Walter over the telephone that you'll hang yourself soon enough, so he'll just wait. They had a real blow-out over you, Callahan. You must be a regular Sundance Kid!" She laughed and turned around to face Alice George who is glaring at us.

***

I go up after class and wait. It has been a long day, and Alice George takes her time sorting out her desk, waiting for the room to empty.

"Matt, Walter Pace came to my home yesterday. We had a long talk. He thinks you could have quite a future."

"My future doesn't look too good to me, Mrs. George."

"Didn't I hear Sally telling you in that stage whisper that you're not going to court?"

"She said the Judge has decided to postpone it. Who knows? Something about he thinks I will screw up anyway, so what's the difference?"

"The difference is you, Matt. *Are* you going to screw up?"

"Probably."

Alice George laughed, I think as much at the tone of my voice as anything. "Matt, you have a powerful friend in Walter Pace. I'm not the only teacher he's been cornering."

"Yeah, he's been talking to everybody."

"Well, Matt, he's a pretty hard man to fool. He's been training residents from the University for twenty years, you know. Walter tells it how it is. A lot of residents who started out planning to be surgeons ended up as pathologists or anesthesiologists. He's what we call a hard grader."

"For some reason he likes me, Mrs. George, and he feels bad about my Dad, but he's off his rocker thinking I'm going to get out from under all of this and go to college or something." I rubbed my cheek. Talking about Walter Pace always made me feel uncomfortable. "And I think he's mixed up about not having his own kid."

"Well, what's wrong with that, Matt? It's no crime having someone care about you."

"Yeah...well, don't count on it, that's all."

"Self pity has killed stronger men than you, Matt." She was stiff, almost angry.

"So why not let me out of here then? I didn't ask for this." I could feel my face harden. I felt a little whiff of the red haze. It scared me.

"Pace wants me to send you over to Mr. Keefer for biology last period," Alice said.

"You mean frogs and that stuff?"

"Yeah, Callahan, frogs and stuff."

"I thought that sort of thing had to wait until you thought I was a good little boy." "

Callahan, I can do anything I want with you people, including kicking you out if I don't like your mouthwash. You want out last period or not?"

"Yeah, sure. I got nothing against frogs."

Loser Makes His Move

I walked out of the building into the September sunshine. The gold and maroon Chief's flag snapped in the fresh breeze at the end of the long side-walk. Over on the fields the teams lined up to begin drills, Coach Ebert's loud sarcastic voice yelled at them that the summer 'holiday' was over. I wished Ebert was yelling at me. All of that seemed a million years ago.

A shadow fell as Loser Swopes slipped up beside me. He was part Indian, always bragging about it. He must have been hanging around waiting for me.

"Hey, Callahan," he said.

"Hey, Loser, how's it going?"

"Man what's this I hear about you knocking out your old man's eyeball?"

I started to walk away.

"Wait a minute! Don't be so damn touchy. What did the Witch want?" He was whining.

"She thinks I should study biology with Keefer the last period."

"Hey, man that's perfect!"

"What are you talking about, Loser?"

"I want you on my team, man."

"What sort of team is that Loser?"

Loser looked over his shoulder like he had a big secret and then jerked his head sideways, so we walked over to a large oak tree at the

47

corner of the school lot. The grass was worn where neighborhood kids played all summer. "We need to talk, Matt," Loser said in a hoarse whisper. I looked around. There wasn't anybody within a hundred feet.

Loser settled himself on his haunches with his back against the tree. He took out a switchblade, opened it and started to snap it into the dirt. "I need some help." Loser brushed back his black hair and looked up at me.

"What kind of help?"

"There are a couple of guys from Detroit…you know. They're bringing grass down to the auto plant. Once in a while they give me a brick to, you know, pass around. Some other stuff as well."

"That's got nothing to do with me."

"People don't like me, Matt. They're afraid. I'm part Indian, like that makes me mean or something." Loser sounded proud. His mind wandered away. He was sweating. He almost stuck the knife into his shoe.

"My granddaddy says we been around Pickreltown since the world was young. Said some of us must have got down into some of those Shawnee villages on the Mad River some moonlight night!"

Loser was watching my face to see if I was impressed. When he saw I wasn't he started whining again. "I need more customers. Everybody around here likes you."

Where did he get *that* idea, I wondered.

"You could make a pile of green," he argued.

"I want nothing to do with drugs."

Loser looked around again to make certain no one was near enough to hear him. "The girl's into it, you know." I stared at him. "Yeah, man, the Judge's daughter," he said slyly.

"Sally Woodruff's running dope?" I asked.

Loser looked smug. "That fat old judge thought it was such a great idea to put Sally in Oz. Like it was some zoo or something. Man, she couldn't wait, you know, to be *real* bad."

Loser flipped unruly black hair out of his face. "The first time I approached her, careful like, she couldn't wait to get in. She does it to spite him. I give her a brick to keep and she makes it up into twenties down in the Judge's basement. Ain't that a kick?" Loser laughed at the thought. "No cops down there, man, nosireee!" He laughed again. Then he looked wistful. "Man would I love to get in those pants!" Loser licked his lips. "She won't have nothin' to do with me. Makes some of those moves that drives me nuts, and then teases me about it." Loser snapped the knife viciously into the dirt. He looked up at me. "You come in, Callahan, you might make something more than bread…know what I mean? I saw what she was doing for you in class,…squirming around like a cat, leaning over and showing you her tits." Loser took a deep breath. "She keeps the books for me too. I ain't too good at figures."

"She's crazy to do any of that," I said. Then something seemed to make sense. "Is she using?" I asked. "She looks strung out."

"Who knows," replied Loser, suddenly wary.

So, it had to be just the way Christina had guessed it that day at the DQ. How was she so sure?

"It's all just junk, anyway. So who cares?"

"Leave me out," I said. "I mean it." I started to walk away.

"The new guy is with me too," argued Loser. "Zinger."

I couldn't believe my ears. "How'd you do that?"

"Oh, that's a long story," Loser replied. "Me and him met at the Department of Youth Services up in Columbus this summer. I had a little problem. They had me on a fourth degree felony offense. Some farmer missed his car out of his barn one morning. The dumb son of a bitch didn't even lock the barn and left the key on the front seat. Was afraid he wouldn't have it when he wanted it, I suppose. Anyway, they couldn't prove nuthin'." Loser paused to concentrate on flipping the knife. Then he continued. "But this Zinger was there too. He was working in the shop where they cut the cars up, and the cops pulled him in. Then some social worker over there in Dayton decided to save his soul by sending him up here. So they let him go. I had to stay for a month." Loser sounded proud. "What a laugh. Anyway, Zinger's going to help.

He's willing to do anything, you know, sell, run the stuff down from Detroit, anything."

Loser looked around again. "Matter of fact, he run a load down from Detroit this weekend. Now he's flashing money around. Those jerks up there better not cut me out! I was the one brought him in. They should'a let me run the stuff."

Loser stood up, wiped the knife on his pants leg and snapped it shut. "By next spring I am out of that classroom and away from that witch. You know what those Detroit guys do? They wear them white coveralls around just like all the other auto workers and the dumb cops don't even look at them. What a gas!"

It all fit. How could Zinger do stuff like that? He just didn't seem like a druggie to me. Wild, yes, but I couldn't believe he was a druggie. Chopping up stolen cars, yeah. But messing with somebody else's brain? I was the stupid one. Letting someone like Zinger get next to me.

"I don't want anything to do with drugs," I repeated. What I was thinking about was Judge Woodruff looking for any excuse to flush me down the toilet.

Loser brushed back his hair and glared at me. "Just think about it, Callahan. Think about that white skin where the tan stops, and all of that green money." Loser's chin was trembling. "And keep your mouth shut. Them Detroit people don't care much for rumors about drugs. That's all they are, you know, just rumors."

The Town Bad Boy

I rode over to school in the mornings with Zinger, but he always took off after school. I wouldn't see him again until after dark when I was walking up Mad River after I was finished at the hardware and was heading for supper at the Red Lantern. Then Zinger would appear out of the shadows, and walk along with me and we would eat together. The waitresses soon caught on, they started flirting with us, especially Zinger when they found he gave as good as he got, which he certainly did. After we ate we would walk up the hill to Seventh Street and I would start my chores. Zinger would just fade off, I would hear him late at night after I was up in my room. He would come up the stairs so silently I usually didn't hear him until he passed my door, even if it was wide open, especially if the television was blaring. He would just be a dark shadow going past. He never came in. Things weren't good with us. We still hung out and all, but I didn't trust him like I did once. I think Zinger knew that. Hell, I'm sure he knew everything, Loser had too big a mouth not to have told him about me. On weekends Zinger was never around at all. Then I worried about him running stuff down from Detroit. Then I would ask myself why that was any of my business, anyway?

Autumn always was my favorite time of the year. It was the football, of course, but I liked it because of the sharp cold mornings with the frost covering the grass, and all of the color, and the leaves underfoot. From the third floor window of Oz I could watch the fields turning color. There was a hundred-acre field of soybeans beyond the stadium that turned yellow as the leaves matured, and now it was a dark brown from the dried bean pods. The nights were cold, it was unusually dry. There would be an early harvest.

The football team was winning. Golden Chief's banners hung from nearly every porch or flagpole. Sally Woodruff had backed off on me, in fact she acted like she hardly knew me. She moved over beside Loser, I could see she was driving him nuts. I thought that was all there was to it, but then I heard Sally and Hank Miller, the new football captain, were getting it on after he ditched his summer girl, Betty Pearce. That was something, since Pearce was supposed to be Sally's best friend. But Sally had plenty of other friends. For my part, I couldn't get her out of my head…guess I really didn't try. Everything she wore made her look better. And there was the perfume. Not much, but I could catch it once in a while. I suppose I wasn't much better off than Loser, just completely forgotten. Even so, there was something wrong. Sally wasn't just nervous, she seemed on the verge of losing it. When she held a sheet of paper you could see how shaky she was. And a nasty temper, but I suppose I am a good one to talk about that. Anyway, after school, Sally went off to cheerleader practice, after which I heard she waited until football practice was over when she picked up Miller in her little blue convertible.

I didn't go to the games. On Friday afternoons I loaded Buck into the back of Walter Pace's old Nissan pickup and we headed for the country wood lot. The first time I drove that truck it was pretty bad. I started it up in the garage and put Buck on the passenger seat and when I got it in reverse it jerked and dumped him on the floor before I got it stopped. Out on the driveway when I started forward, it jumped ahead and I had to jam on the brake to keep from hitting the basketball stanchion. That knocked Buck off the seat again. Buck climbed back up and shoved his butt up against the back of the seat and wouldn't look at me. He just stared out of the window.

Out at the wood lot I slept under the open sky wrapped in a down L.L. Bean sleeping bag. I brought food the girls made up for me at the Red Lantern and I warmed it up over a fire of wood I had cut and split myself. It made me feel really good. There wasn't anything like the red haze and it made me think maybe there was nothing wrong with me. I dreamed about Sally Woodruff.

On Saturdays I harvested hickory and ash with a chain saw and on Sundays I split it with a gasoline splitter that Walter Pace kept in a small lean-to barn. Then I hauled it to Seventh Street, stacked it outside the library and covered it with a tarpaulin. By the middle of October, I was hard as a rock from all of that. And still I dreamed of Sally Woodruff.

Every day after school I hiked down Lake Street and then down Main to the hardware store. The last week of October I was walking along, minding my own business, when Christina George skated up. The kid was always on those damn skates. She swirled around me on the sidewalk and screeched to a stop.

"Practice over early?" I asked. I had to admit she looked great. She wore a pleated maroon and gold cheerleader skirt, and the maroon sweater with the "B" on the front and the big Indian head on the back. "Mom just kicked me off the squad!" she announced triumphantly. When she smiled the braces on her upper teeth glinted in the sun. She was flushed from hard skating. "We'd just started practice, and Sally Woodruff mouthed off at Mom and then turned around and used some filthy language about her, so I walked up to Sally and told her I was going to kick her ass. She made some smart remark, so I smacked her. We were rolling around on the ground and slugging each other. Then the football players pulled us apart, and Mom fired me on the spot. Boy was she *mad* at me!"

I had to laugh. "Keep that up and you will be up in Oz with the rest of us," I said.

"She wouldn't have me. Boy, I'm afraid to go home, if she's still that mad, my Dad is going to tan my hide for sure." She stopped and looked at me. "How old do you have to be before spanking is assault with a deadly weapon or something?"

"I'll bet five bucks you haven't been spanked since you were in the first grade, if ever. That's what is missing."

"You're no help, Matt Callahan." She skated ahead several feet and snapped into a spin of about three revolutions, and then in one quick push was beside me again. "Anyway, I've decided I'm going to skate home with you every day. That's what I should have been doing all along. If I had thought about that I would have slugged her sooner. You need protection, Callahan. That football captain, Miller, is a troll. He won't last with Miss America past the last game." I could tell that had sort of slipped out. Christina wanted to change the subject. "You want to see my scar, Callahan?" she demanded. She hiked up the skirt…considerably more than necessary. "It itches sometimes."

"If you've been showing that thing off in the hallways, Christina, you're going to get a detention."

"Anyway, Sally has your number," Christina argued. "Can't you see she's a mess, Matt? What's wrong with you? Is it true?"

"Is what true, Christina?"

"About her having your number?"

"Yeah, we're talking marriage," I sneered.

Christina made a face at me, then stumbled backwards over a crack in the sidewalk and nearly fell. "I think she's in some kind of big trouble," she said.

"You have a big nose."

"And you have blinders on. Do you think my scar is ugly?"

"The scar will heal, Christina, and the leg is terrific."

That did it. She whirled around, skated away, pirouetted twice and came storming back. "Now *that*, Matt, is the sort of stuff I like to hear!"

I had to laugh. She made me feel good. Not very many people I could think of considered I had a special relationship with them, even if she was just a kid.

When we came to the hardware, Christina did several more swirls and finally skated off. Howard Emerson glared through his new window as she skated away.

I went into the store and walked over to the register to see if Emerson had left any messages, usually complaints, for me to read. Then I checked the shelves and re-stocked where necessary from the storeroom in the basement. Then I swept the floors and finally the sidewalk in front of the store. Mothers would draw their children close or move them to the other side of the sidewalk. I was the town bad boy. They knew it. I knew it.

One Too Many

School nights I liked best. After walking up the hill in the darkness I would go to the kennel, feed Buck, sometimes talking to him about the day. If the hay in the kennel was mashed down I scooped it up with a hay fork and threw it into the back of the pickup. Then I would throw in a fresh quarter-bale for Buck to scratch up to his satisfaction. Then out into the gloom of the yard among the huge oak trees where I would search about with a flashlight cleaning up, and Buck would go off into the darkness depositing more.

After that we opened the side door to the library and hauled in the night's supply of wood, stacking several logs on the blackened andirons. I made a teepee of shavings and kindling beneath them and set them ablaze. Buck would watch every move as if it was the first time he had ever seen it. When the fire flared up, he would groan and curl up on the hearth. If I thought he needed an aspirin I would get one from the bottle sitting beside Dr. Pace's whiskey decanter, pull Buck's mouth open and stick the pill as far back on his tongue as I could. After I learned how to do it right, he would swallow, look at me funny, and thump his tail on the hearth. Then I would have to go to the kitchen and wash my hands.

By the time the fire was blazing , Dr. Pace had usually arrived home from the hospital, showered, and hurried into the library dressed in pajamas and an old corduroy field jacket. He would select several books or journals, pick up his whiskey decanter, fill a shot glass and settle into the leather chair by the fireside. There were very few telephone calls. The calls that did come were very short, unless Pace got mad. A nurse explained to Zinger and me one night at the Red Lantern they drew lots to find out who it was that had to call him.

Most of my time was spent at the long table at the back of the library. Very little was said. It always ended in an argument. Most of the time all I could see was the back of the chair except when Pace threw a journal on the floor. Some nights he read four of those things. I took a look at one of them. It looked like Greek to me. I did learn the books were in sections, I could find anything I wanted to know once I got the hang of it. It made short work of the study assignments. Particularly the stuff Keefer assigned; there must have been ten biology and comparative anatomy books there. Keefer was beginning to look at me strangely when he called on me.

"One of the probation officers called me at the hospital," Pace said from the depths of the chair. I didn't like the sound of that, so I got up and went to stand beside Buck and face Walter Pace. "She said someone called her several weeks ago from the trailer park and said you were over there."

"I was over there before I moved in here. I haven't been back."

"The probation officer went over to your trailer and asked Flora Jean about it and got cussed out for her trouble." Walter Pace smiled and took a sip of whiskey. "I don't think she is going back to visit too soon."

"I don't care what they think."

"That makes two of us. I always liked your mother. She had all kinds of spunk for such a fragile girl." There was a long pause while the fire crackled. Buck whined in his sleep and his feet twitched. "Chasing squirrels," commented the doctor, taking another sip of whiskey. "Matt, if you work hard, you can get out of this hell-hole you find yourself in. But time's getting short. If you relax, they'll dust you off, sure as I sit here." I didn't answer. I felt a twinge of the red haze.

"You just plain don't like anybody telling you anything, do you, Matt?"

"I don't see where you have any right to think you own me or can give me orders," I replied, more bitter than I really meant. But I had been back at that library table every school night since I moved in. What gave him any right to lecture me if I'd held up my end? It was the same exact tone as Howard Emerson used when he lectured me. Whether I did it the way he said or not. It never made any difference.

"I'm getting a little tired of some of the people in this town." Walter Pace rubbed his chest and grimaced. I wanted to ask why he did that, but he waved his hand at me not to interrupt. "You may think this is some sort of rescue mission for underprivileged boys, Matt. That's bullshit. This is no charity event." He started to rub again but caught himself. "I'm out to get even. You're going to do it for me. I'm a gambler, Matt, and you're my long shot. I'm going to show Judge Woodruff, and Erimina, and for that matter, those silly social workers, who knows what about horseflesh in this town, and you're the horse. As far as my ordering you around goes, nobody ever won a horse race by kissing the horse's ass." He filled the shot glass again. He'd had one too many. Definitely. I wondered if *he* was seeing some sort of red haze. I threw my books in the knapsack and ran upstairs and turned the television loud enough to be heard a block away.

I saw the light come on in the kennel as Buck was put to bed. Several minutes later the door to my room opened slowly, and the doctor stood there, swaying slightly, finally putting one hand on the door frame to steady himself. "There's a cemetery up at the top of the hill, Matt," he said. He looked happy for some reason. "Why don't you see if you can get all the corpses up?" He turned and went back down toward his room chuckling to himself.

"Why haven't you ever tried to help Zinger?" I shouted after him. "What's wrong with trying to help Zinger!"

Pace re-appeared at the doorway. "I don't back losers, Matt. Waste of time."

The Female Coyote

I didn't see Walter Pace the next day, or the one after that, which was Friday. I didn't see Zinger either, which was fine with me, I didn't feel like seeing anybody. I told Christina to bug off on the way to the hardware, and she looked like I'd whipped her. I asked Emerson if I could leave early. He just shrugged his shoulders. As if I had ever asked for any favor before.

I went up to the Red Lantern, ate a burger and some hash browns and had them fix up a bunch of breakfast food, milk, and sandwiches; then ran up the hill, put Buck in the truck and went off to the woods. By the time we got there it was pitch dark and I crawled in the bag. Buck laid down on top of it. He always did that, to get warm, or to get closer. Don't know which. Anyway, it felt good even if I was squashed by morning. The next day I was awake at daybreak, the squirrels chattered everywhere. I cut wood all day, only stopped long enough to eat. By afternoon all of the food was gone.

I drank out of a spring on the back of the place even though Pace had told me not to do that. By dark I was so tired from lugging that chain-saw around I had trouble standing up. I sagged down by the fire, stirring the coals as Buck sat opposite me, watching what I was doing. Car lights flicked on the tree trunks long before I saw the Lincoln inching its way up the narrow trail. The engine stopped and Walter Pace stepped out. Buck ran over to him.

"It was sort of quiet back home," Pace said simply. "Do you mind a visit?"

"I'm glad you came out, Dr. Pace." I wanted to say more, but nothing seemed right. I wanted to tell him I was a real jerk. But I guess he knew that well enough.

"I brought extra food, thought you might run short."

Right on! I was starved. And he knew! I had no idea how he would know that. He carried a big frying pan to the fireside, kicked aside a couple of burning logs with the toe of his boot and settled it on the coals. He went back to the car, shrugged out of his heavy red makinaw and returned with a slab of bacon, a carton of eggs, and a coffee pot. He pulled the bacon strips off of the slab and lined them up across the pan. They started to sizzle. I never smelled anything so good.

"Get the canteen from the car," he ordered. When I returned he filled the coffee pot and shoved it among the coals. "You forgot the fork, and the coffee was beside the canteen," he said sarcastically. No wonder he needs two or three nurses to get anything done. When I came back, he measured the coffee by dumping it into the pot until he was satisfied and then flipped down the lid. His expression was hard to read as he watched me in the firelight.

"I'm used to kicking a lot of ass, particularly youngsters who think they want to be surgeons. You have any idea how tough they have to be to do that sort of thing well?"

I shook my head.

"It's not physically tough, Matt, or not-caring tough, it's the idea you might hurt somebody really bad by something you do. Somebody who has trusted you and never did anything at all to you. And that happens. And when it does, you better be plenty tough." He turned the strips of bacon with the long-handled fork. "You're that kind of tough, Matt, if I can just get you there. I'm not kidding you or anybody else, you have the makings. You're smart, you're honest, and you're sure as hell tough."

"Dr. Pace, I have something bad wrong with me." I blurted it out. It sounded ugly in all that silence. My face tightened up.

Walter Pace stopped cooking. "What on earth are you talking about, Matt? "

"I get mad and black out…or something."

"Tell me about it."

"That's it. It seems like a red haze is around me and time seems to stop, and things happen. Then it's all over and it can be good or bad, but I can't change it if I wanted to."

"You ever have a fit, or pass out?"

"No, it's not like that. If anything I feel really good, or really alert or alive or something, I can't explain it."

Pace turned the bacon again. He poured out some grease from the pan and dumped in six eggs, paused, and put in two more. My mouth was watering.

"There's nothing wrong with you, Matt," Pace said finally. "That's simply the last piece of the puzzle. I've heard about opera singers who claim that every time the music starts they go into a state like that, and the opera is as real as reality itself. Champion golfers say the same thing. It's a form of concentration or focus. Something of a gift, although it can be learned to a degree. I've never known a really good surgeon who was not in such a state until the case is nearly over. Time simply does not exist. *Your* focus is driven by anger and frustration. You'll learn to control it, my boy." He didn't seem to have the least doubt. He was either very sure of himself, or he was a very good liar.

We ate the eight eggs between us, and all the bacon, and toasted the bread in the skillet and dipped it in the coffee. We sat and talked. He told me about my Dad. Things nobody ever bothered to tell me. Of course I knew my Dad pitched for the Chief's baseball team, but not that Harold George was the catcher, or that they went up to Columbus to the State Tournament and finished second to Westerville South. Or that he had a baseball autographed by Pete Rose after the Reds won the

World Series. I never saw that baseball. All that stuff made me feel bad. How could I miss someone that much when I was only two years old when he died? It didn't make any sense. It hurt even worse when Walter Pace told me how much my Dad loved me. He said my Dad was always bragging about me whenever Walter saw him down in the rail yard.

Pace alternated between watching my face in the firelight, and staring at the embers. "Matt," he said, "I've been thinking about your 'red haze'. I think we better go up to the University on Monday and have a look in at the hospital. It's time for you to take a look at the other side of the moon. Know what I mean?"

"Not exactly."

"There's a world out there you know absolutely nothing about, Matt, like only a handful of astronauts have ever seen the other side of the moon. There are men and women who use your 'red haze' every day of their lives. I think you need to have a look." Pace stood up. "Yep, that's what we'll do. I'll cancel my schedule Monday and we will run up to Columbus."

Just like that. Just like always. Why did it always piss me off when he talked like that? Like he called all of the shots and what I thought didn't count for anything? It also scared me. Why was Walter Pace always in such a hurry where I was concerned?

It must have been past midnight when he left. I rolled into the sleeping bag and went sound asleep.

A very strange thing happened in the morning. I heard Buck give a soft growl, more felt it through the bag than heard it. It was just daylight. Across the clearing a huge female coyote faced us. Large yellow eyes gleamed in the dimness. A massive brownish ruff and thick white fur. She sniffed the air. She was hungry; probably had a litter back in the woods. Buck tensed beside me. When I sat up, the coyote growled and ran off.

It seemed like a good omen to me. Good luck. I packed up a big load of wood and headed for town. For the first time in a long time everything was going to work out.

The Burn Ward

Monday morning sparkled like a new penny as we zoomed along the freeway in the shiny Lincoln. They were harvesting corn in the fields and the highway was crowded with huge grain trucks. After Marysville I was on new ground. We played Marysville in my first year of high school, before I was kicked off of the team. That's as far as I ever got, so all the freeways and stuff around Columbus really blew my mind. I don't think Walter Pace even noticed.

"Then there's the matter of commitment, Matt," he said. Another lecture. "You remember what I said about the horse race?"

"Yes sir." I was determined I wasn't going to blow up at him.

He looked over at me, swerving into the other lane which resulted in a loud blast from a huge truck. "Matt, why don't you call me by my first name?"

"I guess I just don't feel too comfortable about that, Dr. Pace."

"Have it your way. Anyway, the only trouble with this particular horse race is that the rest of the horses left about four years ago. Know what I mean?"

"I've tried to tell you that, Dr. Pace."

He continued as if he didn't hear me. "Most young people who end up in medicine have had somebody interested in them for years. Not rich people or anything like that…although that doesn't hurt a damn bit…but people who get those kids *turned on*, Matt. It's too long a haul

65

otherwise. It won't happen if you don't commit. You *must* do this, Matt, and soon. Nobody can do it for you." He sounded frustrated. I didn't say anything. I wasn't going to make any promises just to please him.

"There's where the Buckeyes play," he said as we sped past the giant horseshoe. "Ebert says you were good enough to be a halfback in there, not a doubt in his mind. And believe me, Matt, that's big-time football." I stared across the river at the mass of concrete. Another busted dream.

The University Hospital was massive and in the surgery suite everybody knew Pace. We were escorted into the surgeon's dressing room where it was apparently old-home week and finally into scrub suits and then up a flight of stairs and into the observation area.

We twisted into a tiny dark room with a row of hard seats surrounding a pyramid of glass covering stainless steel lights shining directly onto an operating table. There were five green-gowned figures crowded around the table, a huge tray of instruments covered the lower portion, drapes covered everything except where they huddled around a dark red cavity. They were sewing something into a mass of quivering dark red flesh. "That's the heart, Matt," Pace said quietly. "On by-pass. He gets his blood from that machine while they work on his heart." White gauze surrounded the field, there was very little blood. Behind the operating table was a machine with red tubes running everywhere and little wheels turning rhythmically. At the upper end was a woman sitting on a stool looking as bored as the man who had shoved the big breathing tube down Christina's throat. She was twisting and fiddling with dials and tubes just the way he had.

Walter Pace fingered a small button on the ledge in front of us. A red light came on above it. "Stanley," he said, "this is Walter Pace. A student and I are looking in for several minutes."

Only one person looked up. He straightened a bit and nodded. He was at least six feet tall and solidly built. His head was completely covered with a white hood, and his eyes glinted around a thing over his eyes that looked like tiny binoculars. His headlamp winked at us. There were crackling sounds as his clothing moved over a microphone.

"Morning, Walter. We're putting in a mitral valve as you see. Hope you will pardon us, it's getting into the silent part." He returned his attention to the open chest. The nurse passed up a small plastic and metal gadget, and they set about swiftly sewing long fine white threads attached to tiny curved needles by reaching out of sight into the chest. The threads were then sewn around the edge of the gadget until it looked like an upside-down parachute. Only the clicking of the instruments broke the silence. A very tall black man worked in perfect timing with the motions of the surgeon on the opposite side of the table and finally the gadget slid down out of sight and the fingers of both men flew as they tied knots far into the hole. A second assistant, a woman, followed every movement of the other two with a long slender plastic tube that kept noisily sucking out small amounts of blood. One nurse at the table passed all of the tools to the men, they flew back and forth so fast I couldn't follow them. When they were finished with a tool they threw it back on the table. A second nurse at the table kept straightening and arranging things and ordering new supplies from a woman who kept flying around in and out of the room getting things. The microphone crackled. "How long we been on by-pass, Ed?" The man at the pumping machine glanced at the wall clock. "Twenty two minutes Dr. Wilson."

"C'mon," said the surgeon to no one in particular, "let's get cracking and get this thing tight and get him off the pump." I didn't see how they could possibly go any faster. I could sense there was a red haze or something like it surrounding all of them. I had a weird feeling as I watched them. I knew they were into something like the red haze, but it was all of them; they weren't alone, as I was when it happens to me.

Walter Pace punched the button again. "We're going to move along, Stan, thanks for the show," he said.

"Glad to oblige you anytime, Walter," said the surgeon. He didn't look up.

We worked our way down a narrow tiled hallway in and out of ten more observation rooms. It was the same in all of them. All business. In one they were working on a woman's breast, they had cut out what Dr. Pace told me was a cancer and were marking the edges with black ink. Dr. Pace said they were trying to save her breast. In one room they were putting in a huge shiny metal socket where a hip had been. That was bloody. There was no panic. There was no shouting or angry words. It wasn't anything like the stuff I'd seen on TV. Those people working in those rooms cared about each other. It was obvious. I wondered what it would be like to be a part of something like that? Have that small tight group care that *you* were one of them? That you could do those things together and someone would be better for it. Just watching them made me feel better.

By the time we made it back to the surgeon's lounge the open-heart team had finished and was waiting for the next case. The surgeon, Stanley Wilson, looked taller without all of the gown and hood, he had sandy hair with a few flecks of gray sprinkled through it and some faded freckles. He started shaking Walter Pace's hand and kidding him about how Pace had jumped all over him when he had spent time with Pace when he was a resident. I realized with a shock that the assistant was Obie Jordan, a slender muscular six-foot-three former wide receiver for the Seahawks who had quit the pros eight years ago and returned to Ohio State to go to medical school. He shook my hand solemnly, I think he was used to people being surprised. The third person on the team, the girl, was really something. She hugged Walter Pace like he was her grandfather and then bounced over to look me up and down. She was about two inches shorter than I am, tousled brown hair a little sweaty at the nape of her neck, and green eyes that were full of the devil. "You medical students get younger every day," she said. Her eyes twinkled.

"I'm still in high school," I admitted.

"If Walter has you in his clutches," she replied, "you might as well just give up and sign up. Save you a lot of trouble."

So, I wasn't the first of Walter Pace's recruits. "Is that what happened to you?" I asked.

"Yep. Minding my own business up in Toledo, made Valedictorian at the U., and before I knew what was happening, Walter was badgering my parents about me going to medical school at Ohio State. I didn't even like Ohio State…you know, football and all. My parents run a bar up there, and I was working part time. They couldn't get Walter out of the place until I made some promises to think about it."

"So you do this every day?"

She laughed. "Hell no," she replied. This is my last week running the sucker for these guys. I'm a third year resident. I'll go on Urology next. When I come back next time, I'll be up a notch. Then somebody else can chase me around with the damn sucker." She paused when she saw the look on my face. "Hey, don't take me serious. I love it. I'm the one who gets to make sure they get out of this place, you know, all the post-op stuff, orders and all. If I leave anything out, those two," she nodded towards the others talking and laughing with Pace, "fix it for me, and then accuse me of being brain-damaged." She laughed again. "Hey, Callahan, I gotta shower before the next case. Look me up in eight years. I'll buy you a beer." She ran off toward the dressing rooms.

Walter Pace walked over to me. "One more stop, Matt, then we'll get some lunch and head for home. You up for it? This might not be much fun."

"Sure." I wondered what he was talking about.

We caught an elevator to the top floor. It was very quiet up there, we walked down past laboratories and huge linen-storage rooms and finally into a long series of glassed-off rooms with corridors between. Several visitors in the corridors looked into the rooms and talked by microphones to persons inside. In the interior all of the people walking around were in what looked like white space suits as they moved in and out of the rooms. There was a musty dark odor despite all of the spotless shiny surfaces and clean linen. It took only a second to realize all of the persons in the beds were horribly burned. It seemed like an acre of black or red or scarred skin, some arms and legs heavily bandaged, some bare and covered with salves. Bright pink blotches where noses or ears had been. Some of the bandages covered even the eyes. My stomach turned over.

We walked quietly down one corridor and Pace stopped beside a room where a boy about my age was stretched out on a bed. His upper body was covered with square patches of skin, which made him look like a pink quilt. The fingers were missing from his right hand, and there was a tube of skin that stretched from the side of his neck that covered his chin. More square patches of skin covered his head. He had no eyebrows. His eyes stared at us and he tried to smile as he recognized Pace. "Howdy Bobbie," said Walter.

"Hi, Dr. Pace," he replied, "What do you think of my new chin?"

"This week?"

"Last Thursday."

"They should have used your armpit, then you would have had to shave."

The boy laughed. Walter Pace turned to me. "Bobbie lives over by West Liberty. His Dad's barn caught fire last year and while the fire department was fighting the fire from the front, Bobbie went around behind and snuck in to save his 4-H calf. Burning hay fell on both of them. Bobby's lucky to be here. We helicoptered him in. He has about eighty thousand dollars worth of new skin on him."

"You going to be a doctor?" Bobbie was looking at me. There was a light in his eyes. It was the way Alice George had looked at me when Christina was in surgery. A very strange feeling came over me. One thing I knew for certain, I wasn't going to disappoint this guy, no matter if it was a lie or what.

"Well, I'm sort of thinking about it," I said softly. The words sounded strange coming out of my mouth, I couldn't believe I was saying them.

***

It was a quiet ride back to Bellefontaine. I felt I'd been trapped, or tricked. We didn't talk about what we had seen. I wanted to tell him how good some of it made me feel, and how it didn't bother me, and particularly how I felt about seeing Bobbie in that bed. But it seemed if I talked I would be making some sort of promise. And I didn't believe any of this. Why should I hope for anything like that? Why didn't he stop forcing something that wasn't ever going to happen? But then I would think about Bobbie. Now *he* had guts. When Pace talks about tough, he ought to talk about somebody like that. Why would Bobbie think I wanted to be a doctor? My head was spinning. Pace startled me out of my daydreaming.

"Not many rich kids make surgeons, Matt," he said.

Didn't this guy ever quit?

"Too much hard work, too many long hours. Very few rich kids have the stomach for it.," he continued. "The few that do usually are fine, you know, their good schools and all," he paused and looked across at me. "Most of us are from pretty ordinary backgrounds, some a lot less than that. Basically it's a blue-collar business. You need to know that."

I didn't reply. We drove home without another word.

Sally Makes Her Move

I must be some sort of poison. First my own mother can't stand the sight of me, and now in class…in Oz, that is…the Witch can't stand me either. Whatever happened to all of that crap about 'never forgetting'? Now I can't do anything right. The only person in the class, other than Zinger, who thinks I am half-way human, is Sally Woodruff.

Today, for no reason I could figure out, Sally moved over beside me, stuffed her bookbag under the seat and started coming on real strong. She has been wearing sweaters since it turned cold, and I swear she has doctored up her bras some way, or has some special kind or something; anyway, I can see where her nipples are as plain as day. In one dark brown sweater I can see the pink color through the weave.

She's razzing me, calling me 'Sundance Kid' or 'Jesse James'. Then she suggests we're Bonnie and Clyde. She talks loud, just like the Witch isn't even standing up there talking, and the Witch glares at me like it's my fault.

Today I'm catching it about Galileo. The Witch assigned him Friday for first hour history today, and when I missed class yesterday, I was so short on time I crapped it out on the computer. I thought it was pretty good.

Not the Witch. Sally had been cutting up ever since we sat down, and the Witch delivered one of her patented glares. Then she cut loose on me. Her voice trembled. "Look at that," she snapped, flicking the paper she held…my paper…"pure Encyclopedia Britannica. Anyone who can spell 'Galileo' can punch two buttons on a computer and copy off something like this. This is not analysis! I asked for *analysis!* History is studied for what it *means!*"

She stepped around her desk and walked to our row. She pushed past Zinger and shoved the paper at me. "Matt, what did Galileo *do* that scared the wits out of the church? The Pope could have cared less that Jupiter had moons around it!"

The Witch's voice then softened considerably. I could see she was trying to get control of herself. Or maybe the look on my face made her feel bad. I was wondering why I had ever bothered to go live up on Seventh Street in the first place. There weren't any computers or encyclopedias or anything else over at Never-Never Land.

The Witch spun around and headed back for her desk. "Never mind," she snapped. "Get out of here! I'm tired of the whole bunch of you!" It was nearly ten minutes before the bell for the lunch hour. There was a mad rush to get out of the door before she changed her mind. "Matt, stay. I want a word with you."

Sally Woodruff watched all of this with cat-like intensity. Her hand slid over onto my arm. "What's really bugging the Witch is me," she hissed. "She hates my guts. This is all about my moving over beside you. Just keep your mouth shut and let her burn."

Sweat broke out on Sally's forehead, and her mouth was twitching. "When she tries to talk to me I just smile, and keep smiling, and it drives her nuts!" Sally's perfume was suddenly very strong, but it was more than that, almost animal. Her flashing yellow eyes reminded me of the hungry coyote. "She's going to take it out on you, believe me." She gave my arm a squeeze and slid out of her seat. She was wearing a blue cashmere sweater and her cheerleader skirt. She stumbled briefly, caught herself, and fell against me. Her breast slid along my cheek and then she was quickly away.

The Witch sat on the edge of her desk, legs crossed at the ankles; she hadn't missed any of Sally's departure.

"I suppose Sally offered a diagnosis," she said sarcastically.

"She's the reason you're so pissed," I accused.

"As I thought," replied Alice George.

"Sally is Hank Miller's girl," I said defensively. "She just moved over. That's all. What's wrong with her wanting to be my friend?" The thought of that perfume mixed with funky female sweat made my mouth dry. "Why is that any of your business?"

The air was turning pink. I pressed my hands tight against my thighs.

"Sally gave Miller the boot a week ago," said the Witch, then smiled at my surprise. "Football season is over," she continued. "Don't you know? Hank is already back in the willing arms of Betty Jean Pearce, and much the wiser." The Witch put both hands gently on my shoulders. "Matt, that girl is in trouble. I've been watching. She's losing weight. Her mind is a million miles away. Her work is terrible. She's bright, but she's losing control. Her handwriting is becoming illegible. Her hands tremble and she drops things. She has outbursts of temper that are uncontrolled."

Alice George paused and stared out of the window. I wondered if I was supposed to leave. When she looked back at me she looked the way she did that night over in the hospital. "Matt, Sally Woodruff is going to take you down with her."

"She thinks you're gunning for her," I replied. The red haze was fading. I remembered Walter Pace said the red haze wasn't all bad, but I didn't believe that. The feeling scared me and I was relieved it was going away.

"I'll admit, Matt that Sally has frustrated me, more than any student I've ever had. Since I'm the teacher and she's the student, the responsibility is mine to understand her and to do something constructive about it," she said slowly, "And, believe me, I know Sally Woodruff. I watched her all of last year. She started playing up to Loser for some reason, and now she has him so screwed up he hardly knows his name. I can't help that. Loser would be screwed up if he was a Benedictine monk. Not you, Matt. You have a chance to get out of all of this. Stay away from that girl!" She took a deep breath.

"She's never done anything at all to me except tell me she's sorry the Judge put me in this class. She's just trying to square that with me."

"Sure she is, Matt," Alice said sarcastically. But she saw how angry I was. I think she realized she was sounding like a fool, or worse, jealous. "All right, Matt. All right. Perhaps you're right." She let her hands drop to her lap. "I'll stay out of your life."

***

Sally sat by herself in the lunchroom. She waved me over as I lifted my tray from the line. She didn't wait for me to say what had happened, I guess she could tell by looking at me. "See," she said, "What did I tell you, it *was* me, wasn't it?" Sally was sweating, staining the neck of her sweater a dark blue, and her pupils were so tight all I saw were her enormous yellow eyes. There was an empty coffee cup in front of her and a smear where she had spilled coffee on the table top.

"Something like that." I started to eat watery soup that looked and tasted like dishwater. Sally leaned forward, grasping my hand and shoving the soup back on the tray where it slopped all over the table. She pressed my hand between hers, and brought it up to her face. She rubbed my knuckles along her cheek. She looked frightened. Her eyes searched over my face. "I wish I had your guts, Matt," she said simply.

"Sally, if there's something wrong, you need to tell the Judge, or somebody. I'm the last one that can help you," I said.

"She told you to stay away, right? Is that what she told you, Matt?" Sally's eyes flashed.

I held up my other hand defensively. "Hold it, Sally, all…"

She slashed at my hand with her nails, raking and drawing blood, then threw the chair away and ran out of the lunchroom. The kids at the next table watched her go, huddled together, then watched me. Before I could stand up, Christina George had dragged up Sally's chair and plopped down in it.

"What do *you* want?" I groaned.

"Matt, don't run after her!" Christina said, "Let her go."

Betty Jean Pearce and a bunch of girls were gawking from across the room and giggling at us. "Matt, listen to me!" insisted Christina.

That did it. First her mother and now the brat. "Christina, leave me *alone!*"

"No." *That* would have been funny if she hadn't looked so serious.

"Christina, I mean it. You're making a fool of yourself."

"Look who's talking," she said sarcastically.

"Try coming back when you grow up." That hurt. I didn't care. I wanted her out of my hair.

Christina stood up and leaned over the table toward me. Tears streamed down her face. She pressed her lips tight and fought for control. I thought she was going to really cut loose. "All right, big man," she said very slowly, "But let me tell you this. I'm more of a woman than you think, and a whole lot more than that red-headed…*slut* ever will be. And you will come to me, Matt Callahan, it will never be the other way around." She jumped up and left me, mad as a scalded cat. I hoped none of those girls said anything to her on the way out. I think Christina George has her own red haze to worry about.

✳✳✳

I couldn't shake my mood. I left school right from biology class, last period, didn't even go back to Oz to get my knapsack and books. Pretty dumb. My coat was there too, and it was getting cold. The wind swept up Lake Street, cars gunned past me, full of kids laughing and cutting up. Several of them laid on the horn. You know, toot the bad guy, blast the sullen son-of-a-bitch who is probably going to end up in prison. Did you hear?… My dad says….!

I became aware of several persistent beeps then a long blast at the curb. The little Mercedes convertible was slowly keeping pace with me. The window slid silently down on the passenger side and Sally leaned over toward it. "Boy are you in another world!" she accused. Then she smiled, which surprised me. But she was the one in the other world, she had been smoking dope...I could smell it.

I had not thought of anyone or anything but her since the lunchroom. The thought she was going to cut me off was all I could think about.

"C'mon, Matt, get in." Sally begged. Was I dreaming? "You look about to freeze." she added, giving a funny little laugh.

I opened the door and slid in. The heater filled the inside with warm air, the window was sliding up. There was a haze of smoke and a roach was stubbed in the ashtray. As I turned toward Sally she took my face in both hands and kissed me hard on the mouth. Her lips were warm, they parted and her tongue danced against my lips. She pulled back. "You *are* freezing!" she said softly, then, "Let's not fight, Matt." Her voice was silky, deeper than I had ever heard it.

I must have looked stupid. I couldn't believe she was doing this, the way my chest was thumping something was going to blow up. She put one hand up to my face again. "You poor guy," she whispered, "I'm going to be the one who treats you right, Matt. You have to believe that."

I wiped my lips with my bandanna. Sally always wore bright red lipstick. I smiled as I tucked it into my back pocket. "I wish you would make up your mind," I said. My voice was shaky and I tried to steady it. I wanted to be cool, but it wasn't a very good act.

Sally was smiling as if she was used to making guys feel that way. I didn't care. I was the one here right now, wasn't I?

Sally turned serious. "I've been thinking. I'm worried about my grades. I suppose you could say the Witch is right. I can't get anything right. I just don't seem to concentrate anymore. The way I'm headed, my SAT's are going to be a disaster." She paused, watching me closely, "Matt, do you suppose we could study together?"

"I'm sure the Judge will love that idea, Sally."

"Old Fatso doesn't have to know," she pouted. "Besides, Walter is sort of my uncle, you know, Francine and my mother are sisters. And I'll bet you're buried every evening in that library while old Walter loads up on the Johnny Walker. So we could both be in there, and the Judge couldn't say anything about that, could he? I mean, suppose we studied really hard? And Uncle Walter couldn't stop you from walking me out to the car, could he?" She sounded like 'Uncle Walter' was some sort of a joke.

"Sally, I don't know how much good it is going to do you to study with me. I'm no brain," I argued.

"Are you kidding? Half the teachers in the school are talking about you, Callahan. I heard old Keefer bragging about you. The Witch is head cheerleader. You would think they wanted to run you for reform school president.... Oh!, Matt, I'm sorry. I didn't mean that, really I didn't." She looked contrite, pouting her lips and putting her right hand on my thigh and pressing hard. The tips of her outer fingers rested on something that wasn't my leg and was hard as a rock. Those fingertips twitched lightly. C'mon Matt," she pleaded, "don't make me beg." All I could think about were those spiky fingertips. If they twitched once more I was done for!

"Sure, why not?" I replied thickly. My tongue was dry.

Sally gunned the motor and screeched away from the curb, cornering the convertible like an Indy car at Main Street, then shot downtown. She stopped the car across from the hardware. Howard Emerson stared at her out of the window. She smiled and waved. He turned away.

"I guess if you come over I can't stop you," I said, knowing it sounded stupid. I was still trying to act cool, but it wasn't working. What might it be like to have her in that warm library, with that funky smell from her body, and those yellow eyes watching me?

"You want to eat dinner together?" she asked. I opened the door and slid out of the seat.

"No, Sally, I eat with Zinger." That helped. That was cool.

She made a face. Seven thirty at Walter's house, then?"

"How about eight. I have a bunch of chores to do." No piece of putty. Not Matt Callahan.

"Fine," she snapped. But she was laughing as she sped off up Main Street, running the stoplight at the corner.

A Ghost From the Past

I was coming down the long central hallway in Walter Pace's home when I heard the chimes of the front doorbell. I could hear some muffled curses from the library, then the oak door opened and he shuffled toward the front door, the heels of his old leather slippers slapping on the hardwood, while he tugged at the ancient corduroy field jacket. He snapped on the porch light, opened the door, and stared at the woman standing before him.

She stood in the dim light surrounded by the November darkness, her soft reddish hair framing her face, white teeth barely visible in the darkness as she smiled up at him. Her jacket was unzipped, showing her full breasts under a tight tee shirt. I know she must have been a living ghost to Pace, so very much the picture of his wife, Francine. The same radiant beauty, deviltry, and defiant toss of her head. Sally licked her upper lip with the tip of her tongue. Pace finally found his voice. "What......," he demanded.

Sally stepped inside and took off the jacket. "Stand aside, Uncle Walter, I'm here to study with Callahan." She pecked him on the cheek. Pace looked like he wanted to wrap his arms around her and bury his face in her hair. He drew back sharply instead.

"Like hell you......,"

Sally pressed her face against his ear. "Come on, Uncle Walter," she whispered, looking past Pace at me and winking. "The boy needs help!

He talks that red-neck talk from the trailer parks. I thought you wanted him to be somebody! He's flat-out flunking English."

First time I had ever heard anything about English, or how I talked. Sally pulled back and used one hand and then the other to smooth the stray hair along the doctor's temples.

Buck trotted down the long hallway, recognized Sally, wagged his tail and pushed his cold nose into her rump. "Buck, stop that," she squealed, pushing him away. She laughed at me watching her. I'd never seen anyone who looked so fresh and full of fun. "You *old bachelors* living here are sure full of funny tricks," Sally giggled. Buck kept wagging his tail as he looked up at her.

Without another word Sally marched into the library, practically skipped over to the long table, and placed her bookbag beside mine. Walter Pace shoved shakily past me and sank into his leather chair. He gulped the shot glass of whiskey and stared into the firelight. I knew the look. He was trying to calm down.

***

For me the evening went so quickly it seemed over in less than ten minutes. Sally, snuggling close, worked studiously on the papers before her, shuffling, scribbling, opening books and slamming them closed. She was so *warm*. Heat radiated from her body, the tee shirt was soaked with sweat under her arms and down the middle of her back and all I could think about was how that skin would look if she stripped it off. She was wearing perfume, very faint, but with the heat it became stronger. I couldn't concentrate. She leaned closer and whispered as if everything was a secret, then waved over toward Pace in his chair and grimaced. She gestured at Buck, trying to get him to come to her, but the dog kept his place by the fire. The firelight made a bright halo at the edges of Buck's yellow fur as he watched her with solemn eyes.

At half-past ten Walter Pace stood up and brushed at the front of the worn corduroy jacket and tugged nervously at a frayed sleeve. "Sally, it's time you went home. If Aaron or your sainted mother hear about this you'd better explain it was your idea. If Matt needs English tutoring, I'll ask Alice George to help. She was the best English teacher we had around here until she was saddled with that reform-school class." Pace hesitated. "Present company excepted, of course."

"Well, Uncle Walter," said Sally acidly, "aren't you the little match-maker though?" Her voice held a touch of menace. Then she controlled herself. "I'm coming back tomorrow night, Uncle Walter."

She snatched up her books, flashing those yellow eyes at me. "Matt, are you going to take me out to the car, or not?" She turned her back on him. I looked between them, all I saw was her stiff back marching off toward the front door and Walter Pace standing there rubbing his chest. He looked befuddled.

"Dr. Pace…" I began, but then I saw whatever I said would be useless. I tried again. "I like her, Dr. Pace," I said.

Pace glared at me and snapped, "You don't know anything, Callahan. All you have on your mind is pussy."

That did it. Screw him. I hurried after Sally.

I ran down the dark sidewalk to the street. I heard the door slam on the convertible, the interior light came on and flicked out. Would she lock me out? I opened the passenger door and jumped in. She faced me, leaning against her door. She was crying.

As I reached for her she quickly shrugged out of her jacket and threw it in the back seat. In a second swift motion she crossed her arms at her waist and pulled the tee shirt over her head. Her underarms gleamed, and when she slid over to me her skin was hot but not dry, my fingers slipped as I held her. She clutched frantically at me. All I could feel was her body, smell her hair and that perfume, and the soft pressure of her lips. It was another world. I'd never been anywhere like it before.

"Matt, I've been waiting for this forever," she said, "I'm yours, Matt." She squirmed and twisted under me, snatching at my clothes. "I'm all yours," she repeated.

I knew this was all wrong. It was dope talking, not a woman who gave a damn about me. This was an alley cat crazy with heat. But I didn't care. I was as bad as she was and just as crazy. The car could have been on fire for all I cared. We got naked and slithered around. The more we slithered the better it was. Sally Woodruff gave as good as she got, and that was plenty.

***

When I went back to the house the lights were out. I opened the front door and Buck was nowhere to be seen. I heard Sally pull quietly away from the curb. I turned at the door and watched her leave. After a block of quiet coasting she gunned it and the the tires squealed in the night as she shot through the four-way stop at Hayes Street.

Showdown

Every night that week things got worse. Sally was wild, baiting Walter Pace with questions from the table, often about her Aunt Francine. I couldn't help feeling sorry for him, she bored in relentlessly, flickering between menace and fear, twisting at her hair with a long finger and its brightly polished nail, or slamming down a book whenever she couldn't find something. The study periods were shorter, and the time in the convertible longer. Which was fine with me.

But Walter Pace had seen enough. "Don't come here tomorrow night, Sally," he said from the depths of his chair on Thursday night. You're no longer welcome." His voice was heavy, it was obvious he had spent the last several hours making up his mind.

"Good for you, even if it does take you a week to make up your mind, Walter," Sally snapped. "Mother is right. I'm sure you bored Aunt Fran to death. You sure as hell bore me. You couldn't pay me to come back in this house."

She stormed out. After one stricken look at Walter Pace, I ran after her. She was racing the motor and flashed me a hateful look as I climbed into the passenger side. "Sally…"

This session wasn't going to be like the others. It was obvious she had no interest. I could see her pulse pounding like a jackhammer under the muscle at the edge of her throat. "Oh, God, Matt, what a mess," she sobbed.

"Sally, what is it? What's going on?"

She changed her mind. "Never mind," she said softly. "Go on, Matt, get out of here." Reluctantly I opened the door. My foot barely touched the curb when she floored the accelerator. I had to twist away and slam the door. She sped off, laying a long patch of rubber.

In the house Walter Pace was waiting for me in the dimness. The door to the library was open, and the red glow of the dying embers flickering on his face as he stood in the hallway, even so he looked as pale as death. "Matt," he said, "This is madness. What can I do or say to bring you to your senses?" There was that edge to his voice that told me whatever I said wasn't going to make any difference.

"I'll tell you, Dr. Pace, what my 'sense' is. Sally's the same as me. She isn't going to get anything from anybody, just like me. Not from you, not from Mrs. George, not even from the Judge or her mother. An outcast just like I am."

"Bullshit, Matt. She's a spoiled brat and she's bad blood. Believe me, I know more about that than you ever will…if you're lucky."

"She's not some animal. She's a human being. She needs me."

"She's not welcome here, Matt. Do both of you understand that?"

"Yes sir. I certainly understand that." The red haze was all around me. Fortunately Buck came padding out of the library and I forced myself to turn and walk him down the hall and out the back door. Usually he wanted a pat before he would go into his kennel. But he shied away, went in, turned around several times and lay down. "You too, Buck?" I asked.

I went out under the oak trees and stood there. I fought the red haze and tried to think of something or someone other than Sally. All I could remember was the way she felt against my body. The way she moaned when I held her. I couldn't think of anything but her soft body and searching lips.

In the black silence there was a solitary buzzing katydid. A last survivor of the frost…must be a really tough one, I thought. A lot of good it will do him. Their noise always made me feel good. Old Keefer, the science teacher, told me they sang like that hoping to find a mate. Too late, buddy, the frost is going to freeze your ass, probably tonight.

I never heard many katydids down at the trailer park. I'm sure they were around, but all the televisions made too much noise to notice them. Late at night, like now, when the televisions were off, the most likely noise would be some drunk swearing, and a woman moaning as he beat her around. That had a special sound in a trailer park late at night, like a piece of meat being slapped down hard on a butcher's block.

Blackmail

The last day of the week was always a mess in Oz, but today was a total disaster. While Zinger and I walked in I asked him if he was going to meet me for supper, since he missed all of last week. I was acting like, was he mad or something? Then I tried to tell him to lay off running up to Detroit, if that was what he was doing. I was worried because Loser was acting strange. Like he had snitched to the cops. He was acting that weird.

But Zinger wasn't interested in any lecture. He stared at me and said, "Mind you own business, Matt," like I was Christina's age.

I went in to class early, hoping to see Sally. She and Loser came in together, arguing. Not even a glance in my direction. Sally left just before noon but not before she and Loser had more angry words.

After the last bell in the afternoon I saw Sally down by the old oak tree at the corner of the lawn having another violent argument with Loser. He had his switch blade out and jabbed angrily at the trunk of the huge tree. When he yelled, grabbing Sally by the shoulder and shaking her, I ran over. Several kids stopped on the sidewalk to watch. Loser glared. "Stay out of this, Callahan," he snarled.

"Fuck you, Loser," I replied, watching him closely. The switchblade snapped into the trunk again. If he shoved that thing in my belly it was going to come out my back side.

"What's going on, Sally?" I asked.

"She is short five K, *that's* what's going on," snapped Loser. "I trust her to keep the money, Miss Rich Bitch and all, and now she's short! A couple of boys from Detroit are coming down here and run some bamboo slivers through her tits, that's what's wrong."

Spittle made a slimy streak down Loser's chin. I remembered the day at the Dairy Queen when that weirdo, McQuirk, shook the sliver of bamboo out of the envelope. Then I watched a dark blue wet spot in Loser's crotch slowly spread down the left leg of his Levis. He was pissing his pants right in front of me!

I turned back to Sally. She seemed smaller. Her eyes were rimmed with tears. "Get lost, Loser," I said. I didn't bother to look at him.

"Well up your's, Callahan," said Loser. "I gave you a chance to help out, but you couldn't see your way. You want to mess in now, go ahead. You'll be the one in the hospital. Those guys don't give a shit about anything. And they particularly don't like being stiffed out of five grand." I could hear the knife snap closed. "You think you're so tough, Callahan; you're not tough, you're trailer-park trash. You get her to come up with that money or I'm going to tell them you and her done it. For all I know you did! They won't care if you did or not; they'll kick it out of you just to see it fly!" I wasn't watching him, I was watching Sally. He gave something that sounded like a sob, then I heard him leave.

"Sally, you running drugs?"

"I don't have anything to do with selling them, Matt."

"Are you using?"

"No." She was lying. She sensed that I knew she was.

"All I ever did was take bricks from Loser and bag it into twenties in my basement. Then I would give it all back to Loser. He wanted me to keep track of the money, so I did. It was kind of fun."

"Well, so…"

There was a long silence while she studied me. She ran her tongue along her upper lip. "So last July I turned on a red light down by K Mart, you know, slid through," she said slowly, "and I hit this kid being pushed by his old man in a stroller. Just coming off of the curb. Didn't hurt anything, the kid screamed all over the place, but was just scared. Of course it wrecked the stroller, the guy was furious, was going to call the cops and all. I had about five hundred of Loser's money stashed in the trunk, and I gave it to him to forget it. He took it."

"And?"

He works over at Kelly's garage. He called a couple of weeks later saying there had been 'additional expenses.'"

"So now he's in you for *five thousand*?"

Sally had stopped sniffling. "Yeah, but it's over, Matt. I told him if he ever called again I was going to the cops."

"You should have told him that a long time ago."

"You don't have Fatso Woodruff for a father."

"So what is it with Loser?"

"Loser says they're sending down two people from Detroit tonight to get their money. He says I have to meet them out at the lake. He says they've told Zinger and him to stay away. Apparently they don't want anyone else around when they talk to me. I suppose one of them will be that little bald creep I smacked in the face at the Dairy Queen."

"You have the money for them?"

"I .. have enough…something, enough they'll leave me alone, I think." Sally's pupils were dilated to where I could barely see the yellow. Her nostrils flared as she talked. She was scared out of her wits. I pulled her over to me and put my arms around her. She clutched at my shirt front trying not to fall. As usual her body was on fire. I pressed her to me and she seemed to steady.

"You can't go out there alone, Sally."

She started to shudder. "Matt, Hank Miller knows about some of this. He knew something was wrong. I asked him to help, he called me a dumb bitch, and said he didn't want anything to do with drugs…or me. I…know you hate drugs. Loser told me. I thought you would tell me to get lost."

"I think I'd better go out there with you."

Sally twisted and pulled away from me. Her expression hardened. "You should stay out of this," she said finally.

"After…those nights we had, you think I should stay out?"

"Matt, whatever they might want from me,…you know…I can handle it. But if you want to be there, I'll make it up to you, I promise."

"You already have, Sally."

"These aren't Boy Scouts, you know."

"Sally those people are going to be a lot more worried about you turning into a snitch than they are about five thousand dollars. You can't go out there alone."

Sally again moistened her upper lip with the tip of her pink tongue. I'd seen her do it many times when she was uncertain. But this was different. It made her look menacing. It didn't seem like Sally. Or more like the Sally who never paid any attention to me, never knew me. Then she said, "If you want to go I'll pick you up at Walter's at eight thirty."

Fight or Die

Sally arrived at eight thirty. Her headlights blinked through the blackness, winking across the beveled glass panes of the front door. I watched her pull to the curb as I came down the last step of the front staircase. I wore heavy gear, canvas pants and a thick red wool shirt. I was jumpy. None of this felt right.

It wasn't who might be out there. Someone was always out there, so what? What was wrong was Sally's lying. She was lying about not using. Was she lying about the money? Was she lying about me?

Walter Pace opened the library door and looked toward the street. "So, Matt, you're going out? What is this, anyway?"

I wanted to tell him it was none of his business. I also knew that whatever I said wasn't going to work. There was no right answer. So now I was lying. "Sally and I have a date."

"In those clothes? What is it, a Paul Bunyon masquerade?" It was very hard to lie to Walter Pace.

"We're going out to the lake."

"To toast marshmallows, I suppose."

I had to laugh, and for a minute I thought he was going to also. To tell you the truth, I really loved that skinny old man. He hated lies.

But Pace was serious. He was rubbing his chest and had that pallor around his mouth. His face twisted. Was it pain or anger? I couldn't tell.

93

"Listen, my boy," he said slowly, "something's wrong here. Don't go out that door."

"Come on, Dr. Pace. You can't order me around. Who do you think I am? I'm not Buck. I'm not your dog. I don't lie down on your hearth and wag my tail just because you say so."

"Matt! Don't do this!"

He was losing it. So was I. Sally laid on the horn from the street.

"I'll be back before midnight, Dr. Pace," I said. "I'll take Buck and go out to the woods tomorrow morning. Sally and I have a date, that's all there is to it."

"Matt, you're lying to me. Don't lie to me!" His voice cracked. Sally honked again. Walter Pace jumped sideways to block the door. "No, I said!"

I shoved him aside and opened the door. One of my hands was on his bony shoulder. There seemed to be no substance to it. "If and when I come back," I snapped, "it'll be when I'm good and ready! You don't own me. Nobody does." I stepped out into the blackness and ran down the sidewalk.

***

The county road toward the lake was so dark in the overcast that Sally had to use her brights to pick out road markers. A thin cold fog misted the windshield, she had the defroster fans on high, and the wipers swept intermittently back and forth. She crept along, looking in the gloom for the narrow grassy road that would lead down to the lake. "This is the only time I ever wished there would be ten other cars out here," Sally said.

We turned in and slowly worked our way back through the thick second growth enclosing the roadway. Bushes scraped the sides of the car. Occasionally the wheels spun in a depression. There had been a lot of rain. The fog layer undulated four feet above the ground. The 'picnic' area came in to view, the lake glistened beyond, gentle waves lapping against the grassy shore. Sally cut the motor and switched off the lights. There was silence and darkness.

"Keep the lights on, Sally," I said. She switched them back on, then nervously reached for the radio. "Leave it off. Lock the windows and doors." Sally pushed the toggles on her arm-rest and there were two comforting clicks.

"Where's the money? " I asked. "Better get it out."

Sally squirmed in her seat. "There isn't any, Matt. Only from last week. Several hundred at best."

"Then what did you mean that you 'had something', Sally? What were you talking about? I couldn't believe what I was hearing.

"There are two large boxes of twenties in the trunk," Sally replied evenly, as if she were addressing a moron. "You see, I always skimmed some from each brick…everybody does, they say. The dealers expect it. They hope the street people will use some of it, sort of makes for a tighter family, you know?"

"You mean you think you can buy these people off with their own drugs? Sally, are you out of your mind? Do you think they would even consider that for a minute?"

"There's a lot more than five thousand dollars worth in street value," snapped Sally. "A lot more. Now they can have every bit of it back and I'm out of it!" She shuddered. "No more. That stupid Loser. No more!" She turned pleading eyes toward me.

I sat bolt upright in my seat. "Sally, start the engine and get the hell out of here. We're going to the cops if I have to hog-tie you!" But as I spoke I knew it was too late. A black pickup had slipped up behind us without lights and two large figures dressed in white coveralls were running up beside the doors.

"Sally get going! Spin this thing! Run over those guys if you have to, just get us out of here!"

A knife ripped through the convertible roof on her side and a white-jacketed arm reached down quickly and snapped the door toggle. The doors on both sides were yanked open and I was thrown onto the wet grass. Before I could move, two huge hands gripped my upper arms, yanked me upright like a paper doll and twisted me to face the lake.

"Don't move, kid. You can watch your girlfriend all you want, but if you try to look at me or move a muscle, you're on your way to the hospital." The hands relaxed and I stood stiffly, surrounded by the dark mist. The beams of the headlights looked firm enough to walk on. My eyes adapted slowly to the darkness.

The other man threw Sally, sniveling and protesting, against the side of the car. He was a head taller than she was and powerfully built. His arms stretched the sleeves of the coveralls. "Where's the money, bitch?" he demanded.

"In…my purse." She nodded at the car. Lights glinted while the man searched around in the car. He took the purse to the headlights, ruffled through it, pulled out a tiny wad of bills and threw the rest on the ground.

"Pick up the purse," said the gruff voice behind me. "We don't want none of that lying around." I glanced back at the pickup. There was a small boat pulled up on the bed. I saw a glint of metal on the boat seat. A length of logging chain. I should know, I had dragged enough of the stuff up from the hardware basement. The man behind me jabbed me hard in the kidney. Felt like the edge of a set of brass knuckles. Pain shot both ways, up to my neck and down between my butt. My knees nearly buckled. I gritted my teeth.

"You call this money?" the man said, gripping Sally's chin in a huge fist, "This ain't even change. You do better than this, girl, or I'll slap your head off."

"In the trunk," she stammered, "there's almost three hundred twenties in the trunk. That's worth more than we owe you! The key is there in the ignition."

"Well, I'll be damned," he exclaimed. He looked over toward the man standing behind me, eyes glinting in the glare from the headlights. He wrenched the zipper of the sweat- stained coveralls down to his waist revealing a massive expanse of black hair over his chest and belly. He grabbed Sally by the neck and ripped off her shirt. She screamed and he slapped her face hard, then reached behind her, pinning her to his chest. "Girly, girly," he said softly, his voice throaty, sounding just like Bo Calloway sounds when he beats Ma around.

"Leave her alone," I said.

I could hear my voice, but it seemed as if someone else was talking. Hard and gritty, full of hate. The man turned toward me, amused. Sally sobbed, cowering back from him. He shoved her roughly. "Get them pants off," he said. "I'll be back as soon as I kick the shit out of your little friend."

He came slowly around in front of the headlights. Sweat poured in ragged streaks through the forest of chest hair. He swayed slightly on his feet…the practiced careful balance of a street fighter. "You'd rather take her place, tough guy?" he demanded.

The red haze was settling. I could barely see him, but I did see his eyes open slightly. It was the only motion he made. He never understood or recognized the quickness. I had already twisted, my hand coming, the back edge hard as tire rubber catching him where his nose joined his upper lip. I felt a crunching sensation jolt up my arm as cartilage collapsed and separated from the bones of his face. Before that blow landed my other fist was on its way, catching him with all of my weight behind it. It snapped his head the other way, there was a loud crack like a branch breaking, and blood spewed into the pale fog. I could see, despite his size, he was going to fall backwards, and I lunged forward. I was going to have his throat in my hands before he hit the ground. But that was not to be.

The big man behind me quickly pinned my arms to my sides, bent backwards, leaving me kicking thin air. I snapped my head back, trying to smash his face, but the old fighter was much too quick to be caught that way. He slammed me to the ground, settled two massive knees on my shoulders, crushing down on my chest and squeezed my face between two muscular thighs.

The wounded man rolled over into a half crouch and shook his head. He cupped his hand under his face, looking surprised at the pool of blood streaming down from his chin and dripping from his neck. "You sonth ub a bidth!," he snarled, like he had a bad cold.

"You buthded my node!" He felt his jaw carefully. "You buthted my jaw...my teed don fid no more!" He staggered to his feet, searched in his jumper pocket, and drew out two long slivers of bamboo. "One of thede in each eyeball, smartass. You'd going to need a seeing-eye dog!" He pressed forward with the first sliver. The vice grip of the legs tightened on the sides of my face.

I watched the mangled face above me, and the needle point of the sliver of bamboo trembling in his hand. He was going to blind me. Then rape Sally. More than that. They would kill us. Of course. The boat. The log chains. Wrapped together, weighted with cement blocks. Sixty feet of still water. I heaved and kicked, but the needle point stabbed for my eye.

A stun grenade went off ten feet away. "**POLICE!**"

Frozen ringing silence.

Then a second grenade went off and the area crawled with men in black uniforms and plastic helmets. "**POLICE!**" They carried sawed-off shotguns with laser sights taped underneath the barrels. I watched a bright red dot center on the white coveralls of the man straddling me. "Stand up slowly asshole," said the cop pointing the shotgun , "or you meet God tonight." Just before the sliver stabbed into my eyeball another man in black kicked bloody-face in the chest, flopping him backwards onto the grass. There he groaned and rolled over. The officer leaned over the fallen man, flipping his limp arms behind his back and snapped cuffs on his wrists.

"Stand up slowly, Matt," said a voice behind me. Jimmy Peters. I obeyed. Peters pushed back the plastic shield covering his sweaty face. "Turn around." The cuffs clicked home. He slipped his finger around the cuffs to check them. "You have the right to remain silent," said Peters sadly. "You have the right to counsel…" He droned on with the Miranda. I could hear it being repeated in several other places. I looked down at my shoes. They were covered with leaves and mud. There was a commotion behind us and a fourth police officer came into the light holding Sally by the arm. "I found this one running down the road screaming like a banshee," he said to no one in particular. When Sally saw Jimmy Peters she ran over to him, threw her arms around him and started sobbing.

"Jimmy! Jimmy! Get me out of here. Get me out of this awful place."

Sally clutched her torn shirt trying to cover herself. She glared at the cop standing beside her who was calling on his handset for a van for the prisoners. Peters stripped off his black nylon SWAT jacket and she slipped it on, giving him a quick smile.

"Matt brought me out here, Jimmy." She turned away from me. "You know…I thought he wanted to make out, I guess." She looked at Peters helplessly. "And then all of *this*." She started sobbing again. "Hush, Sally," said Peters.

"There's more, Jimmy," she said quietly, glancing quickly at me. "Before we started Matt took several boxes from Pace's dog kennel and we put the stuff in the trunk."

"That's a lie!" I shouted. Suddenly it was very quiet. Several of the cops turned and stared at me. Jimmy Peters walked over and stood in front of me. He didn't look like my friend any more.

"Matt, we've been watching these two goons for three months. Every time they came to town. We have a snitch who tells us you and your buddy Zinger are the local bag men. Now I'm questioning a witness at a crime scene. If you interfere, we can add obstruction of justice if you like. One more outburst and that's exactly what will happen."

He turned his back on me and walked back to Sally.

"What exactly did you put in the trunk of your car, Sally?" he asked.

"Drugs, I think, Jimmy. Grass in sandwich bags, I guess."

"You didn't know this was a drug drop? Is that what you're telling me, Sally?"

"No. I swear it Jimmy."

"Sally, either you're a liar or a complete fool. The Judge is going to skin you alive."

"Are you going to arrest me?"

"Of course not. We know where to find you. I'm taking you home. The Judge needs to know about this."

Sally started crying again. As they walked past me Peters hesitated, as if to give me a chance to say something. It was a waste of his time. I wasn't saying anything. My world had crashed into a million pieces.

***

The prisoner van approached the clearing, its cherry-top spinning and the headlights flashing back and forth for no particular reason. "Charlie," said Peters, "take Callahan in and put him in the detention cell. Keep him away from any adults. I'm going to take Sally home and then I'll be down. Get tow-trucks in here for that convertible and the pickup. Take them in and impound them as evidence. We'll go over them in the morning."

As he walked past me, he paused and shook his head. "I can't believe this, Matt. You're going to break that old man's heart."

He turned away taking Sally with him. She looked at me over her shoulder. The look said she loved me. Phony! All phony. What was it with her anyway? Peters would be lucky to get her home before she found some excuse to take off that jacket. That made me jealous. It wasn't my turn any longer, was it? It was Jimmy Peters' turn, even on the way home if that was what he wanted, I could see the way she squeezed against his arm as they went past.

If they had thrown us in the lake, at least I would have been the last one. And they would have said we ran off together. Consolation prize. The guy who finally ended up with Sally Woodruff.

A hand on my head pushed me into the back seat of the cruiser. The other cruisers and the van were already inching back down the long muddy lane. Before we reached the road I saw a small pinprick of light from a tiny pencil flashlight sweep over the empty convertible. It flashed along the grass and leaves and up under the bottom of the car. It danced back and forth on the trees and blackberry stalks and finally back toward the muddy road. The light flashed upward briefly. I saw the small serious face and the thick-lensed glasses of Harold McQuirk.

Jail

The juvenile detention lock-up was beside the office and across from a wall of bars that created the first barrier to the jail proper. The arresting officer entered my name on a sheet behind the counter, selected a key from a box, unlocked the door and led me inside. His hand rested steadily on my elbow, there was not going to be any surprise from any sudden move. He removed the cuffs.

"Take off your belt and shoes."

He backed off when I bent over. This was a very careful cop.

"Leave them on the floor and move back." He picked them up and went out the door. Several seconds later he opened the door and handed me a pair of worn black plastic clogs.

The room smelled of Lysol, cigarette smoke, and stale sweat. A steel bunk with a bare mattress was welded to one wall, a metal table with two chrome chairs were in the opposite corner. A separate room without a door contained a toilet and steel sink. Between the room and the office was a small square of smoky glass.

I stripped off my heavy woolen shirt and rolled it up for a pillow. The black blanket folded over the foot of the mattress had heavy nylon strips woven through it in both directions, I guess so I couldn't tear it up and hang myself. I lay down on the cot and closed my eyes.

All I saw were dirty white coveralls and a bamboo stiletto jabbing toward my eye. What lies were being told to Sally's parents? Why wouldn't

Jimmy Peters listen to me? Who was the snitch? That one was easy…that stupid Loser. A thick wire grate covered the ceiling light. It blazed down on me with haloes of orange and yellow around it.

***

I startled awake, no idea of where I was. Showers ran and men swore. Metal trays clanged. Back to reality. How could I possibly have slept all night after what happened?

A woman jailer in a neat uniform brought in plastic containers on a tray. A pile of cold scrambled eggs, two greasy sausages and a tepid cup of coffee. A toothbrush and small bar of soap lay beside it. "No razor, kid," she announced pleasantly, "you need to shave, you tap on my wall and I'll bring in a razor and watch you. If you want a shower you'll have to wait until the big boys finish." She smiled and left.

I ate the food and then went into the toilet. Was she was watching me through that stupid one-way mirror? It took a long time to get a stream started. As soon as the noise of the showers stopped on the wall beside me, I signaled I was ready for a cleanup.

At mid-morning there was a tap on my door and Alice George walked in wearing gray wool shorts with a scarlet stripe in the seams, running shoes, and an Ohio State jacket. A sweatband held back her dark brown hair. Saturday morning, I realized suddenly. No school. I'd obviously interrupted the Witch's morning exercise. She smelled like cold air and deodorant. "You need clean clothes," she said, inspecting me. "Are your things out at Pace's"

I nodded.

"Upstairs?"

"Top of the stairs. Middle bedroom."

"The place is crawling with cops. But I'll get you some stuff." She sat down. "We have to talk."

"I'm not saying anything to anybody." My voice was tight.

"Matt, I know you. I know a lot of kids. I'll bet my job you're not a ringleader in this. There comes a time when you have to save yourself. I hope you know that."

I sat down across from her. In the worst way I didn't want her to get mad and leave. Just seeing her sit there was all I wanted. I wanted time to stop.

But something was terribly wrong. She was looking at me and fighting back tears. A sickening sensation came over me; somehow this wasn't about me. She was having trouble getting the words out.

"Matt, Doctor Pace is dead," she said. She reached across for me, but I jerked back.

"He died last night. The police found him in his chair in the library last night."

Time did stop. I remember looking up at the light in the ceiling, the haloes dancing around it. I felt myself sliding off of the chair. Everything went black.

***

Alice George was bending over me, crying. I was stretched out on the floor and my tee shirt was soaking wet. The jailer held a bucket of water. I shook my head and tried to sit up. The blackness swept back over, but I fought it off and after several seconds I grabbed the edge of the seat and climbed back up and sat down. Alice George glared at the jailer, who ignored her.

"They do this all of the time," she said over her shoulder as she went out the door.

"I'm sorry, Matt," Alice said. I could hardly hear her. All I could think about was that poor old man who tried to help me and all I did was hurt him. Jimmy Peters was right. I broke his heart. A terrible pain wrenched across my chest. I wondered if it was that kind of pain Dr. Pace was feeling when he rubbed his chest. My stomach heaved. Then I was sick. I scrambled over to the toilet and threw up the sausages. I snatched a handful of toilet paper and shakily wiped my mouth. I tried taking some deep breaths. I stood up. I had puked down the front of the tee shirt before I made it to the toilet.

"You better leave, Mrs. George," I said, "But if I had to hear this, I'd rather hear it from you than anybody. Now I want to be alone. I'll be all right."

All I could think of was Loser calling me 'trailer-park trash'. Alice George didn't need to be around trailer-park trash.

She wasn't finished. "Matt, do you know a man named Jerome Hayes? A lawyer?"

"I remember a man out at Seventh Street one Friday night before I left with Buck for the wood lot. Tall with gray-hair. All business. He is…. was…a friend of Dr. Pace."

"Matt, he's a very important man," Alice began. "More than a friend to Dr. Pace, he handled all of his legal affairs. He's also the Governor's principle aid and legal advisor. He's waiting outside to see you. Just arrived. He's been up at the house. Now he's out at the desk arranging for me to go into the house and get some clothes for you." She paused when she saw my face tighten. "Matt! Stop this. You need help."

"He can help all he wants, but I'm not saying anything against anybody. Nobody can make me."

Alice George stood up. Disgusted, I think.

"One more thing, Matt, they picked up Zinger and Loser last night on U.S. 75 near Toledo," she said quietly. "Apparently they were running. Matt, if you persist in this noble silence you'll be left holding a very heavy bag. I don't want that. Can't you understand? Do you have any idea how much I care?"

She threw a newspaper on the table. Zinger stared innocently from the front page. Loser held his hands in front of his face; his idea, I suppose, of how the Mafia would do it.

Alice walked over to me. I wanted to back away, I knew I must smell like the rest of the place, only fresher. She put both arms around me. "Matt, you stubborn Irishman, what am I ever going to do with you?" And she hugged me hard, just as hard as she did when she was worried about Christina. It felt real. It was real. I grabbed her and hugged her back. She was all I had and I didn't want to let her go. But then I thought about Dr. Pace, and I let go. All I do is hurt people. Alice smiled. I think she knew.

F. Jerome Hayes was still all business. He handed me his card and told me he was going to 'represent' me, whatever that meant. "I don't have any money," I said.

Hayes smiled. He had iron-gray hair carefully combed, a ruddy complexion and bright blue eyes. "I'm sorry about Walter," he said briefly, "fine man. We were friends for years." He didn't sound all that broken up, but I'm not a lawyer.

"What can you tell me about last night, Matt?" he asked.

"Nothing…sir."

"Out of some misplaced sense of loyalty, Matt? Or is there a *good* reason?"

"I'm not a snitch. I won't be responsible for anyone going to jail. I don't care who they are. I may be trailer-park trash to you, but I don't snitch."

Hayes was unimpressed. He sat down carefully, placing an expensive soft brown leather briefcase on the floor…after he had inspected the coffee rings on the steel table. "I don't understand the part about trailer parks, Matt, but do you have any idea how many times I've heard clients talk about loyalty, while in the next room his buddy is busy spilling his guts, usually lies, so the wrong man ends up going to jail?" He paused to see if any of this was sinking in. I glared at him, but he was really scaring me. He fished around in the briefcase.

"Matt, there is a grand jury meeting up in Detroit Monday. A very big deal. You're nothing. Just a sideshow in all of this. So they're moving things here quickly to meet that schedule. Judge Woodruff has had to recuse himself…that means take himself off of the case… because of the fact of Sally being a…witness."

Hayes paused and looked at me sharply. When I didn't blink, he continued. "Judge Frederick Harding is going to sit in on your hearing Monday. He is coming up from Champaign County. "You better make up your mind in a hurry whether you're going to save yourself. By Tuesday it may be too late. The show will be up in Federal Court up in Detroit. Do you want to talk to the ATF people about what you know?"

"No."

"Then Matt, you must answer one question for me if I am to represent you. It's confidential. It cannot ever be used as evidence against anybody. Are you involved in any way with the drug trade? In any way whatsoever?"

"No sir. I am not."

"Then sign this piece of paper. It says I'm your attorney until you see fit to fire me."

"I think I like the way you do business, Mr. Hayes, but you're wasting your time."

But I was bluffing. For the first time since Sally Woodruff had stabbed me in the back I felt a slight glimmer of hope. This guy was for real. He acted bored but I didn't buy it. If Walter Pace liked him, he was no phony. Pain stabbed back into my chest. Walter Pace was gone, wasn't he? And I walked out on him. And now I was going to pay; Aaron Woodruff would see to that; Aaron Woodruff who hated me. And Walter Pace was gone. So much for any hope.

Hayes smiled. "There will be no fee, Matt. We call it *pro bono*. It is what we lawyers do when we start to feel guilty about making too much money. I will see you in court on Monday."

Juvenile Court

I was taken from the detention cell over to the Logan County Courthouse on Monday morning, wearing jeans, my Nikes, and a light blue oxford button-down dress shirt that still had the purchase tags on it when Alice George handed it to me the day before. I suppose the innocent baby blue color was her idea. The jeans folded underneath were fresh laundered, still warm from the dryer.

It was cold and windy but I had my heavy waxed cotton hunting coat. The cop parked in front of the broad sidewalk, turned on the cherry light, unlocked the back doors and came around to let me out. Howard Emerson watched through his window. Several people on the sidewalk and in the crosswalk stopped to rubberneck. Emerson said something toward the back of the store and then turned back as he watched me. He was laughing.

"Come on, Callahan," said the cop, "you're causing a traffic jam." She glanced over at the onlookers. "They never get enough," she said sarcastically. She took my arm and marched me past the statue of Chief Blue Jacket toward the old stone building.

She was trying to make it easy on me but she was also careless. She had refused to cuff me at the jail and now her holster was two inches from my hand. The red haze started to swirl. I could have had that gun and flipped her on her butt before she took another step. I gritted my teeth. The red darkened, there were sparkles of light all over her uniform. She seemed to

109

sense something and turned toward me. Her hand moved toward the holster. It would have been far too late. As the red mist swirled I had seen someone…Bobbie, the burned boy. And behind him in the distant mist Walter Pace smiled at me. Then as quickly as it came, the haze faded. "Relax," I said, "I'm not going to run."

A bailiff met us at the top of the wide sandstone steps, shaking his head sadly as he snapped a cuff on my wrist, squeezing the opposite cuff in a big hairy fist. "Ginny, don't you know these kids will run on you?" he demanded. I knew he had watched me coming up the walkway. He was large and gray and paunchy, but he knew something about red haze.

"And we're not allowed to shoot 'em no more." He looked at me and grinned. Some joke.

"Good luck, kid," said the lady cop, and she left.

Then F. Jerome Hayes took charge of me. That was the end of the cuffs. "Changed your mind, Matt?" he asked. He wore a dark charcoal suit with a faint white pinstripe, a white shirt and a blue silk tie with bright orange spots. He carried his soft leather briefcase. Not a hair was out of place. I shook my head to answer his question.

We entered the darkened courtroom. It smelled like fresh wax and old mildew and dust. The ceiling was high, covered with metal squares with patterns printed on it. The windows went to the ceiling letting in the gray light. I could see gnarled tree branches outside waving in the stiff wind. Where would I be now if I had run for it? It would be better than living in a cage. Even dead.

A court stenographer came in, seated herself at a table facing us and fussed with her equipment. She glanced across where we sat in front of the massive judge's bench, studied lawyer Hayes carefully, then returned her attention to me…curious: Mr. Keefer, my biology teacher, looks that way when someone brings him a new bug.

A shaft of light from the hallway flashed as the tall doors opened and Sally Woodruff and her parents arrived. She wore a cream-colored dress with a high waistline and a lace collar. The fully pleated skirt fell well below her knees. Silk stockings, dark brown pumps with low heels. Her dark red hair was piled neatly on her head, no lipstick. She looked like a choir girl. She smiled at me. Judge Woodruff glared at me and steered her firmly into a row of seats on the opposite side of the room.

Someone turned on the lights in the room. "Just look forward, Matt," said Hayes. "As soon as everybody is here, the judge will be in." He opened his briefcase and pulled out a cell phone. He turned away from me, punched at it and started talking on it. I couldn't hear what he was saying. F. Jerome Hayes was a busy man.

Sure enough, the large bailiff appeared through a side door and shouted. "Hear yez! Hear Yez! The Juvenile Court of Logan County is in session! The Honorable Frederick W. Harding presiding." He was followed by the judge in his flowing black robe, a short man with a shock of windblown white hair. He seated himself and looked us over. He had a ruddy complexion, a lot of wrinkles around his eyes, and a firm mouth and strong chin. He whacked the gavel once as if he was testing it out.

"This is a juvenile hearing," the judge announced in a voice that was better suited for talking over a cement mixer. "This is not a trial. I will ask most of the questions. I am permitting three attorneys in here who will represent several persons." Judge Harding nodded in the direction of the Woodruff family. "John Butterworth will represent Miss Woodruff. Miss Woodruff is a witness in this hearing, she is not accused of any crime. Mr. Butterworth, your remarks will be limited to Miss Woodruff's testimony and matters related to it, and that only. Do you understand, sir?"

Butterworth was new in town, I had seen him in and out of the hardware. He was always sucking up to Howard Emerson. "Yes, Your Honor," said Butterworth. Now he was sucking up to the judge as well.

The judge turned his attention to the center of the courtroom. "You are Capilletti?" he asked a slender young man sitting in the first row.

The attorney stood up. "Yes, Judge, Anthony Capilletti. I represent the two adults who were arrested here Friday night. And held in jail since then, I might add."

The judge ignored the remark. He turned to us. "Where are the boy's parents, Mr. Hayes?"

Jerome Hayes adjusted his tie briefly. "I spoke to them Saturday afternoon as soon as I was retained by my client, Judge. Both declined to be here today. The step-father was particularly emphatic about the matter."

The judge's eyes bored into me. "How do you feel about that, Mr. Callahan? Do you think you can have a fair hearing without any parent present?"

I shrugged my shoulders. That pissed him off. "Mr. Callahan, this is not a dumb-show. The stenographer cannot record body language. You have a right to have a parent here. Do you wish to insist on that right?"

"No sir. I didn't ask for them to be here. I don't want them here." That wasn't true, I would have given a lot to see Ma in back of me.

"Very well," replied the Judge. "Mr. Hayes, you may cross-examine any one of the witnesses, even though the others may not cross-examine your client, do you understand?"

"Yes, Your Honor."

Harding shuffled some papers on his desk. "Where are the arresting officers?" he asked irritably. "I don't see them here. Why aren't they here?" I wondered if he always asked two or three questions at once.

The bailiff snapped upright from where he leaned against the wall. "They're on their way over, Your Honor. They're bringing the adults. They'll be right here!" He hurried up the side aisle and out of the door into the hallway.

"Good," said Harding to no one in particular, since the bailiff was no longer in the room.

"Mr. Capilletti, I'm going to deal with your clients first. I understand they are under indictment and are due in Detroit, is that correct?"

There was some scuffling and clatter as the two prisoners were brought down the center aisle of the courtroom by Jimmy Peters, a second cop, and the bailiff. Their handcuffs were removed as they stood silently before the bench. They wore the same white coveralls, which were even more grimy. The man who tried to blind me wore a huge bandage over his nose, held in place by a strap behind his neck. Dark blue rings surrounded both eye sockets. Even his eyelids were dark blue. He looked like a giant raccoon. His lip curled when he saw me. I thought raccoon-face was going to come after me…judge, cops, bailiff, and all. Boy was I hoping. The first thing I was going to do was knock off that silly bandage.

The second man faced the judge, looking like a giant statue. He was really a whopper. No wonder he tossed me around like a bale of straw. His hair was gray, and his ears were scarred and deformed. His cheekbones had been beaten flat a long time ago. He was relaxed, he wasn't mad at anyone.

"Very well," said Harding. He nodded his head at the man with the bandage. "Let's get you sworn in and hear what you have to say, mister."

Capilletti stepped in front of the prisoner. "Your Honor," he began, his voice smooth and soft, "Mr. Jervis can't speak. His jaws were wired shut Saturday morning by an oral surgeon in Columbus. He has a fractured jaw. In addition, I have advised both of my clients not to speak in this courtroom. They are under federal indictment, and I plead, with great respect, your Honor, that they not testify here until we have them relieved of all of those charges. It could cause them great harm to be forced to testify. They will take the Fifth if that is what you require."

"Even greater harm if I find them in contempt."

"Certainly, your honor. And they would be very happy to stay here as long as you wish while you work that out with the federal judge," he added slyly.

Harding stared sullenly at the trio. Then he motioned to the bailiff. "Get them out of here!" he snapped. They were hurried back up the aisle. Raccoon-face glowered at me as long as he could. "No need to worry about him," said Jerome Hayes in my ear. "They're going away for quite a spell." But that wasn't what I was thinking. I was thinking I would like to be out at that lake again with that other big jerk somewhere else, so I could have another crack at raccoon-face.

"Very well," said Harding, regaining his composure. He signaled to a chair beside the bench. "Now Sally, I want you to come up here and take the oath, and then sit down and tell me what happened out at the lake on Friday."

Sally took her time. John Butterfield patted her shoulder as she excused herself past him, and then followed her like a puppy and stood beside her as she was sworn in. She sat facing the judge and us, crossing her legs demurely at her ankles. Then she looked across at me, gave me a big smile and looked up at the judge, still smiling. She never looked this way in school. There was no sweating or nervousness. Was it all an act? *Which* act? Where was the real Sally? Was there one?

"Sally," asked Harding, "that was your car out at the lake on Friday night, so you did the driving? You had a date with Matt?" Two questions.

"No, sir, it's my mother's car," replied Sally.

"All right. So you had a date?"

"I…guess so.." she began.

"Well, did you or didn't you?" asked Harding.

"Sally," chimed in Butterworth. "It's all right to have a date, just go ahead and tell the judge the truth."

Sally looked up at Judge Harding. "Well," said Sally, hesitating, "he wanted me to pick him up. I…thought it was a date." Sally twisted a handkerchief in her lap. "We'd been studying together all week over at my Uncle Walter Pace's home. I really got to know him doing that, and I thought he just wanted to go out…you know, go get a burger or something." Her voice trailed off.

There was silence except for the soft tapping of the court stenographer's machine. I realized I was finished. I would have believed her myself if I didn't know better. It was hopeless. I was the one doing the fighting. I was the one Loser wanted to nail. I was the one who was violent.

"And?" Harding was very gentle.

"When I got there, Matt and Uncle Walter had just had some sort of big fight. I think Matt was getting kicked out or something. As soon as we left the house Matt ran around to the kennel, you know, the dog kennel? You can stand up in the front part where there is hay and stuff."

"And?"

"There were cardboard boxes full of plastic packages."

"Like the packets over there on the table?"

Sally hesitated. Butterfield's voice coaxed again. "Go ahead, Sally, go over and take a good look. You can walk over if you wish."

"No, I can see from here. They're the same. Matt carried them out and put them in the trunk of my mother's car."

"Why did you agree to go out to the lake?" asked the judge. "Did Mathew Callahan know those men were coming?"

"I…think so," stammered Sally.

"Did he say they were coming?"

"No sir."

"Well then, how would you know?"

"He was acting real funny. Like it really wasn't a date, you know."

Judge Harding looked across to F. Jerome Hayes, who was talking on the cell phone again. When Hayes saw the Judge's stare, he jumped, hung up and straightened his tie.

"Attorney Hayes," said the judge pointedly, "Do you wish to cross-examine that statement?".

Hayes looked surprised. "Why no, Your Honor," he replied simply. "We know there were drugs in the car. We admit there were drugs there."

Harding's eyes narrowed. He turned back to Sally. "Sally, the police tell me your shirt was ripped off. Who did that to you?"

"That man who was just in here. The one with the bandage. He was awful!"

"Is that when Matt started fighting?"

Sally shook her head. "No. Matt was joking around with them. I think he had me out there to, you know, sort of take their mind off of being mad at him or something. The fighting started over money."

She started to cry, wiping her eyes with the handkerchief. Butterfield reached over and patted her arm. I couldn't believe what I was hearing. I wanted to jump up and shout, or throw something, anything but sit there and listen to those lies.

I felt Jerome Hayes' firm grip on my arm. He squeezed so hard I knew it was going to leave a mark. "Matt," he whispered in a very threatening tone, "sit still. If you ever did anything right in your life, do it now. Sit right where you are and remain quiet." But I was teetering on the brink of the red haze.

"So they didn't fight over you Sally, is that what you're telling me?"

I think I was supposed to be there instead of the money only it didn't work." They didn't fight over me. Matt owed them."

Aaron Woodruff sprang from his seat like he was going to charge across the courtroom. Harding banged the gavel hard. "Sit down, Aaron," he shouted. Then he turned his attention to my table again. What he saw made him turn purple around his cheeks and red over the rest of his face and forehead. He started shouting again, louder if anything. "Councillor! If I see you on that telephone again, I'm going to hold you in contempt!"

Hayes snapped the case shut. "I'm very sorry, Your Honor," he apologized.

"Attorney Hayes, please approach the bench," snapped Harding. It was supposed to be for privacy, but Harding was far too upset, I could hear everything he said. Harding obviously didn't care.

"When are you going to start *defending* this boy, councillor? Are you trying to make this look like a railroad job by a country hick judge so you can get it thrown out on appeal? If so, Hayes, you are making one hell of a mistake." Harding was furious.

"I certainly beg you pardon, Your Honor, if my courtroom strategy is irritating you," said Hayes, "and I mean no offense, but unless you are going to seek to remove me for cause, I must insist on conducting my defense in what I consider to be my client's best interest." Hayes sounded as if he were lecturing a first-year law clerk.

Harding's face turned an even brighter red. His eyebrows shot up, causing deep wrinkles in his forehead. "We'll see about that!" he snapped.

There was a long silence during which Butterfield nodded to Sally and she got up slowly, glanced over at me and then walked back beyond the gate in the bar and sat down between her parents. She didn't bother to smile this time.

Harding took a deep breath. "I have the police report," he said to the courtroom in general. "It seems pretty straightforward. Does anybody want to see it?" He looked across to our table. When Jerome Hayes just stared at him, Judge Harding shrugged his shoulders. Then the judge concentrated on me. "Now, Matt, it's your turn. I want you to come up, be sworn, and take a seat and we will hear your side of the story." His voice was kind. I felt sorry for him for what was about to happen.

F. Jerome Hayes stood up at the table. "I very much regret, your honor, that Mr. Callahan refuses to testify. That is his prerogative, of course, but I'm afraid it might be seen as prejudicial. It should not, in fairness, be taken that way. He even refuses to discuss this matter with me." Hayes turned his palms upright and shrugged his shoulders.

There was a long silence in the courtroom. I think the judge was waiting for me to speak, or at least look at him. I don't really know. I was staring straight ahead at the wall behind the bench.

"Well, that about does it," Harding said in a tired voice.

Hayes held up a hand. "Your Honor, if I may…" Harding nodded at him disgustedly.

"Your Honor is aware that there is a grand jury being seated in Detroit today. There are two persons who have finished there, and presently are on their way here. I hoped they would be here now. They landed in a private jet at the Bellefontaine airport ten minutes ago. I beg your indulgence for just a few more minutes?"

But there was no need for Harding to reply. The huge double doors to the courtroom groaned open. Two men entered, a slender black man, and a nearly bald man in a black suit wearing thick glasses, stepping carefully as he stared down at his shoes to be certain of his footing. The black man moved with the easy grace of a mountain lion.

Zinger! I hardly recognized him. His hair was cut very short and even. He was clean-shaven, wearing a dark-striped gray business suit, a snowy button-down shirt and rep tie. Harold McQuirk held a wrapped package the size of a small book in both hands. They sat down in the front row behind the bar.

"Who are these people?" demanded the judge.

"May I approach the bench?" Jerome Hayes asked politely. The judge nodded.

The judge leaned toward the sleek gray-haired attorney. More stage whispers for everyone to hear.

"The younger man is an FBI undercover agent, Your Honor," explained Jerome Hayes, "one of the best they have in interstate drug trafficking."

Harding stared at Zinger who looked straight ahead at the center of the judge's bench.

"The other man, named McQuirk, is a special agent ATF on loan to Detroit. They tell me he is some sort of legend in their agency, no one ever takes him seriously until it's too late," Hayes finished proudly.

"So?" asked Judge Harding.

"So McQuirk has had a tape recorder stuck under the Woodruff car and wired to the radio speaker for over three months. What you have heard for testimony this morning has been a massive amount of perjury and the bearing of false witness against an innocent boy. I suggest we listen to this tape before we are all labeled for participating in a farce of total lies."

Sally screamed. A shriek like a wounded animal. "Lies! Lies!" she screamed at the top of her voice. "That man tried to feel me up in the Dairy Queen, ask anybody! Ask Matt! Oh God, ask Matt or somebody!" She started to sob uncontrollably.

Both Butterworth and her father reached for her but she fought them off and rushed toward McQuirk. I have never seen anything like it. The maddened coyote eyes were yellow and blazed with hatred. Her lips were pulled back in a snarl, teeth bared, tongue jerking in and out in a wicked red point. She tore at her hair with her hands as she charged.

A face straight from hell. Finally a glimpse of the real Sally Woodruff. I never want another look as long as I live. Jimmy Peters tackled her before she got to McQuirk. I swear she would have torn him to pieces.

F. Jerome Hayes turned back from the bench and faced me, a satisfied smile on his face. I'm sure my mouth was hanging open. I was numb from my forehead to my toes. He gripped both of my arms gently and eased me down into my seat.

***

The Judge asked for identification from McQuirk and Zinger, and then had a tape recorder brought in. McQuirk explained in a dry voice that the tape was edited from over forty hours, but that the originals were available. Sally didn't have to listen. She was half-pushed, half-carried out of the courtroom by her mother.

The tapes were embarrassing, all the heavy breathing and threshing around in the convertible when it was parked in front of Walter Pace's house. If they were editing, why didn't they edit that?

Aaron Woodruff glowered alternately at McQuirk and Judge Harding as the tapes started with Loser and Sally arguing over money.

There were several episodes with Miller in the convertible with Sally…which made me sick. Sally didn't use much imagination. She used all the same lines. "Oh God, Hank I have been waiting for this forever!" I put my hands over my ears.

But Aaron Woodruff had a worse time. He began to wheeze, and every time Sally moaned in the convertible he wheezed louder. I wondered if he had ever had to use an inhaler like Ma uses every day?

Finally, the lake. All of it was there, Sally's lies, even the zipper going down on the coveralls, then the fight, and the stun grenades which overwhelmed the system momentarily. Even some of the Miranda warnings, and snatches of Sally's appeal to Jimmy Peters for help. Aaron Woodruff objected at the beginning, jumping up from his seat and sputtering, "Entrapment. This is entrapment. This is not…"

"Aaron, sit down! snapped Harding.

The edited tape ran for over an hour. Each segment was identified by McQuirk's dry voice. There were several segments in which Zinger participated, always subtly identifying himself and the time and place in the conversations. Zinger was always warning someone about getting caught or about arrest and its consequences, for which the others heaped scorn on him. Judge Harding ordered the tape stopped at that point.

"I suppose you consider this to be your consenting party to these tapes?" he asked McQuirk.

"Yes, Your Honor," replied McQuirk.

"It's entrapment!," said Woodruff again from the corner of the room. "It can never be admitted as evidence."

"We think those segments can be admitted," said McQuirk.

Judge Harding told Zinger to stand up. "Who is this man?" he asked McQuirk.

"His name is Thomas Jefferson Alexander," replied McQuirk. "He graduated from Princeton three years ago, *cum laude*. His father is on the faculty there. In his second year of college he spent a summer with the FBI as a clerk, kept pushing them for undercover work and they finally started using him. He got the nickname 'Zinger' in the Bureau because he never misses. Last year, at the urging of the Director, he applied to Harvard Law School and was accepted, but then this thing in Detroit started to look as if it could be turned so he asked for a year's delay and it was granted. We planted him in that chop shop in Dayton and he worked his way in. He has made it in pretty far in Detroit on weekends acting as a courier. As far as I'm concerned this is his last job, he's getting too old for kid stuff. He's going to get himself killed."

McQuirk paused while he removed the tape from the machine and carefully re-wrapped it. He seemed to be in no hurry. "But I will say this, Your Honor, I will bet you when he gets out of law school he will be back in government service."

"You little bastard," wheezed Woodruff jumping up from his seat, "you're not going to put my girl in prison!" The bailiff moved toward Woodruff.

"We don't want Sally in prison, Woodruff," snapped McQuirk. "We want her to testify in court. The truth. Everything she ever heard about this drug ring. She either sings like a canary or she's toast. I promise you that. We want the people in Detroit. Sally and that stupid Loser can start it turning. We'll roll those two other goons easily enough and it will go like rotten dominoes until we have who we want. We're not interested in small fry. You can take care of the perjury and whatever else down here. We want Sally in Detroit in Federal Court. We want her there without any fancy maneuvers. Want her ready to be worked over by some big-time criminal lawyers. And we don't want any more lies."

McQuirk no longer looked like a helpless rabbit. He looked like a ferret going in for the kill. "Something else, Woodruff, in case you're interested," he said quietly, "an agent will be at your home with a search warrant when you get there. We want to vacuum your basement. I know you think it's clean as a pin. We have some pictures taken through a basement window of your wife cleaning up. We also have the sweeper contents from your trash can. If I can get anyone to accept any of this as evidence, I am going to have you before the discipline committee of the Ohio Supreme Court."

Aaron Woodruff slumped down heavily in his chair. I felt sorry for the fat old man. She still belonged to him. She had him. And she was destroying him. I was walking away. Not without a lot of damage. But I was walking away.

Judge Harding removed his glasses and rubbed his eyes. He replaced them and stared down at his two hands placed flat on the desk top. Then he banged the gavel. "This court is adjourned."

One on One

McQuirk darted up the aisle as soon as the Judge had dismissed the court. Jerome Hayes filed papers carefully into the proper dividers of his briefcase. He interrupted me when I tried to thank him.

"Never mind that, Matt," he said quickly. "You and I have some business to do out at Walter Pace's house, and I need to be back in Columbus as soon as possible. I have to get some things signed here. I've asked your friend, Alexander, to take you out there. I'll be right along. Now be a good fellow and let me finish up here."

He turned away, motioning to the court stenographer.

Outside the courthouse Zinger honked from the row of head-in parking on Columbus Street as he gunned the engine of a small gray rental car. The door swung open for me.

"Hop in, bro," Zinger said cheerfully. He seemed in very high spirits. "Leave anything over there?" he asked, tipping his head back toward the jail.

"Only nightmares," I replied. "Alice George brought me these clothes. She took the rest. I hope she burned them."

"How true, how true," said Zinger philosophically. He backed out and headed east on Columbus Street.

"Zinger I can't stand thinking about Dr. Pace. How he must have felt dying. I walked out on him." I turned toward the window so Zinger couldn't see my face.

123

"Callahan, for a bright guy you can be remarkably stupid."

"What does that mean?"

"Walter Pace knew everything that was coming down. What he didn't know for sure he guessed. He loved you, Matt. He knew you'd be back. You have to know that. I don't think for a minute that Walter Pace believed a word of my cover. He took one good look at me that night in Never-Never Land when he asked how old I was. And then I made that stupid remark about a Rhodes scholarship. I had never made a slip like that before. Walter saw through my cover then and there. He never said another word. Never offered to find me a job or asked where I was going. Everyone in the county knows finding jobs for people like me was one of his hobbies. No, old Dr. Pace knew what I was, and he knew I wouldn't live in his house and eat his food if I was after you. Even a government snitch wouldn't stoop that low."

Zinger slowed the car while a small boy retrieved a soccer ball from the street. "The deduction, therefore, as Sherlock Holmes would say, is that Walter had both of us pegged right from scratch. You for a head made out of solid marble, and me for a Federal snoop.

We drove along in silence. "While we are having 'true confessions', Matt, want me to tell you where I blew this case? So bad I need some serious down time, or even out altogether?"

"Sure."

"When I heard about the log chain and cement blocks in that boat, I realized you and Sally were never supposed to come back from that lake. They were going to drown the two of you. I misjudged that. I'm going to really catch it back at the Bureau and I deserve it. Only thing good about this mess was watching Mr. Big in Detroit drop a load when he saw *me* on the witness stand this morning!"

"That's what I figured, Zinger, when I saw that length of chain. No one would have known we had been out there. Two runaways. Just disappeared. The car never found."

"Right on."

Zinger pulled to the curb in front of the Pace home. "I'll tell you something else, Matt. I was over in the gym several weeks ago and that George girl appears out of nowhere and starts in on me to play her some one-on-one, saying I couldn't hack it and all that.

So I give her a game, and you know what that kid is doing? Trying to pump me about you. That's what the whole thing was about. Every time I picked up the basketball it was what did you like to eat? What movies? What music? She was talking about people I never heard of. She makes me realize I'm getting too old for this game. Talk about blowing my cover! If she had been in some of those meetings in Detroit I would be floating in the river up there now.

Jerome Hayes' Cadillac swished past us into the driveway. Hayes was in a hurry. Zinger reached his fist over toward me.

"See you down the road, bro," he said. Zinger's brown eyes glistened. "If you had wanted in, Matt, I wouldn't have kept you out. It isn't like that. You want to be a druggie, I'm gonna take you down. When it comes to getting your ass shot off in some alley, or going to prison, you don't have any friends, man. Remember that. Every man gets to choose his own poison."

He laughed, showing those white teeth the waitresses were so nuts about. "Let me know bro if you ever want to go undercover...I got the connections!"

He drove off laughing at my stupid stare.

Inside the house it was bitter cold. Jerome Hayes was shuffling papers in the library, arranging them in neat piles along the back table. Gray ashes had blown out onto the hearth from a pile between the andirons. Walter Pace's shot glass lay on its side where it had rolled to the edge of the table and rested against the arm of his chair. I placed it exactly where I used to watch his long thin fingers alternately lift it for a sip, slowly place it down, and turn a page.

"Matt, I need some signatures," Hayes said. Then he realized how abrupt he sounded. "Sorry," he said, "sit down, Matt."

Jerome Hayes took a deep breath. "Matt, Dr. Pace made a lot of money and spent very little of it. No hobbies, no vices."

Hayes sounded disappointed. "He left it all to the hospital, quite a sum. But he left this house to you, the woodlot in the country, and enough in a trust to take care of it. The condition is that you care for Buck until he dies. Then it is yours in fee...that means it's all yours to do with as you please, including selling it if you wish."

Hayes took another slow breath. It was obvious he was enjoying himself. "In addition," he continued, "he set up a another trust, I am the trustee, to cover your college expenses if and when you ever reach that blessed condition. I am the sole judge of what is a reasonable expense. In addition he put one hundred thousand dollars into a certificate of deposit to be cashed and belong to you if and when you should ever happen to matriculate in a medical school. I thought that was a terrible idea. Did my best to talk him out of it. But you know Walter. He was absolutely convinced you will become a physician. I will have to say, however, he was sound in mind when he did it. I can assure you it would be of no use for anyone to challenge what he wanted you to inherit."

"I can't believe any of this."

"Believe it, my boy."

"I don't deserve this. We had a terrible fight the night he died. He would want to change it."

Hayes smiled. "One of the nice things about being a lawyer, Matt, is that we don't have to worry about what might have been. We deal with what is. I advise you to do the same thing. And please remember that I control the money at the present time, you do not. You do have the house. You want to burn it down after I leave, go ahead. And please sign the papers where the red plastic tabs are stuck."

Hayes extended his hand. "See you soon, Matt. I'm late for Columbus. Mail the papers to me after you read them." He paused. "And get a driver's license. I checked. You don't have one." He hurried away.

Buck Takes a Walk

I sat all afternoon in Walter Pace's chair watching the shadows move slowly along the walls. I was cold and numb. I tried to call up the red haze but nothing happened. Was it gone forever? I tried to remember everything Dr. Pace had ever said to me and why he had said it. That helped a bit. I didn't touch the papers. I thought about burning them.

I walked out back and fed Buck, but it didn't help. I crawled inside the cage and hugged the big dog. He sat there looking at me, expecting me to take him somewhere in the truck. When I didn't move he lay down heavily against me. I sagged back against the plywood wall and tried to make sense out of it all. Nothing made sense except that I was very tired.

It was turning dark when I woke up. I crawled out of the pen and brushed away the hay. Back inside the house I stared again at the papers. Then I pulled on my heavy coat and walked out. I let Buck out and started walking. He followed , wagging his tail. He was having fun. I wasn't.

I shoved my hands deep into the coat pockets. We wandered slowly along Mad River Drive and finally along Rt. 68 where it started down the hill toward the lights of downtown. When I realized where I was going I walked faster. We passed large old homes, most past their prime, with small circular flower-beds around huge old trees, flowers wilted and browned by the frost. I turned up the cement walk to the George home. Tree roots had made the sidewalk cracked and uneven.

Christina's roller-blades lay haphazardly on the porch. I picked them up and pressed the doorbell.

About the Author

The author is an honors graduate of Harvard Medical School and was trained in surgery at the Massachusetts General Hospital in Boston, Massachusetts. He lives and works in rural Ohio.